THE
POWER
OF HOPE

Written by Crew RF-1

Daniella Lainez
Hannah Gregory
Ryann Stidham
Saramarie White

Under the direction of Alladia Patterson,
Anna Glovin and Written Out Loud Studios

Cover design by Naomi Giddings

**Written
Out Loud**

This book is dedicated to all the loving parents and supporters of this crew, and to each other.

CONTENTS

THE
POWER
OF HOPE

CHAPTER 1:
A New Beginning

As he placed the light cardboard box full of his faded baggy clothes onto the dark unwelcoming depths of the moving van, Seth felt a strong twinge of regret. He would never come back to this quaint countryside house surrounded by once beautiful blooming flowers and crystal clear streams. He would now be moving into the small urban town which would take one long menacing hour to arrive at his apartment. He had always wished to live a normal life, normal friends, normal parents, normal characteristics, and most importantly, a normal school. But the only time he had ever gotten close to this point is when he was just settling in from middle school and he had two kind best friends- Liam and Elijah, and he fit in perfectly well at his old school. He also didn't have to see his parents very often as instead he had a nanny.

His nanny/housekeeper, Marilyn, was probably the best thing that happened to him. She was very understanding and always made sure the kitchen smelled like warm homemade cookies whenever he came back from school. Marilyn also congratulated him when he was moved up a grade because it became expected that he correct the math teacher in classes or sometimes even teach them himself! It also became a routine that he basically wrote novels whenever a writing assignment came up.

Marilyn saw something special in the boy and never stopped encouraging him that sometime everyone would recognize his abilities. But when his parents lost all their money gambling, Marilyn had to go, and so did all his happiness. With the house empty all day and the TV on all night, the place became torture to live in. The surrounding flowers' brightness and colour seemed to die away and dust collected in every corner and crevice. They now began to eat take out every night and he grew so skinny that even the teachers made sure he ate four helpings every meal. His once almost content life turned upside down so quickly into a thoroughly miserable one.

Lazy. That's what his parents were. Lazy, selfish, unsuccessful, greedy, rude, devil like, and all the other mean words you could ever call someone would surely fit his parents personalities. Maybe the awful life started when his parents realized he wasn't a girl like they wanted. He seriously had to wear pink shirts and onesies saying things like 'im a princess' and 'girl power' before they finally started dressing him in boys clothing (which didn't happen for a long time). He wondered what his life would be like if he was a girl.

He brushed aside some strands of tangled ginger hair which was blocking his view and made a mental note to put hair gel in that spot next time so it would keep back the annoying always messy mane.

Or maybe he could do that now.

So Seth rushed to the now-sparkling bathroom and swiftly opened the bathroom cabinet. A wave of disappointment swept over him as he scanned the empty shelves of the cabinet and sighed. He must have already packed the gel in the toiletry bag.

Oh well, things don't always go as you want them to.

He slammed the wooden doors shut and glanced into the chipped mirror. You could plainly see that the ginger haired boy was in desperate need for a good trim and brush. His hair was completely out of hand! Underneath the jungle of ginger were forest green glasses perched on a freckle covered prominent nose. His large monkey-like ears stuck out of his mane of hair in a really embarrassing way and Seth tiresley tried to hide them. His long slim arms were hanging loosely at his sides and he just realized how weird they must look- doing absolutely nothing. The thought only just occurred to him that if his parents found out he wasn't packing then he would be in big trouble, when his dad himself burst into the room.

"What are you doing boy- the television hasn't been packed yet!"

"I was... Packing the toiletry bag!" He added a little too enthusiastically.

His father eyed him suspiciously then added

"Remember boy if you annoy your mom and me on the drive-"

"I'll get grounded for a month without any entertainment. I know."

He interrupted carelessly, ignoring his father's menacing glare and his stubby finger barely touching his nose. So with one last look of deepest loathing, the ginger haired overweight figure of his dad thumped downstairs.

Great. I haven't even finished packing my books and now I've got another urgent matter dumped on my list.

A few hours later, the family of three were bobbing across town in their old dusty pickup truck. They were just passing the school Seth would go to once summer break was over and he took a large gulp of air to calm down his nerves. There were children playing in the playground and a group of boys challenging a soccer match. The sign reading 'WALLOWDALE HIGH SCHOOL' shone brighter than ever in the sparkling summer sun welcoming all visitors to a so called "fun day" at the school. A group of girls were walking past laughing their heads off to someone's joke. But Seth saw one girl who was trailing behind staring at the ground. He couldn't make out what she looked like in the bright sun, but he could tell she didn't want to be there. Maybe he wouldn't be the only one not fitting in.

"Are you up?" Her mother called through the door. Hope woke up, on her back. After a couple blinks, the dream, though still unpleasant, had departed. But not the anxious feeling it left her with. It had found companionship with the discontentment that appeared when she turned over and noticed her cast. Brochures were laid out on her desk, seeming to take up the whole space. Every college with a swim scholarship. As if taking on the advanced classes wasn't enough. *Sleep on it,* her mother said. *Then think about it in the morning.* She thought about it. Although she didn't sleep on it, as much as toss and turn. She could barely keep her eyes open while she threw on a faded old Red Hot Chili Peppers t-shirt, struggled to get it over her cast, and then put on a pair of jeans she had lying on the floor of her closet. "Yeah. I'm up".

"Good. You have a very busy day today." Her mother said, before starting downstairs.

Hope turned to face the door, all those brochures in the back of her mind. Over the last weeks, they had made a very comfortable home there. *Why do I even have to worry about this right now? I'm not even halfway through Junior year.* Before she would have welcomed a disruption to her morning routine, but now she prayed for it. The stairs creaked on her way down, and she could hear Nolan mumbling something about sleep-deprivation. Hope wondered how her brother could be standing around in the shockingly cold linoleum kitchen and still be thinking about sleep. He was fumbling with frozen waffles when she came into the kitchen. Her mother was standing next to the microwave, checking her calendar book. "Nolan, do you have any idea when your science club starts meeting?" Nolan inserted both waffles into toaster slots, and turned the knob up to an agreeable three. "No." He said "Despite the science club's constant presence in my life," he looked back at his mother, irritated. "They haven't told me anything." Nolan noticed Hope, reflected the tired look on her face, and handed her the cereal box from the cabinet. They seemed to have a mutual agreement to help each other through the mornings. Especially now that she was one handed. She sat down at the table and started eating. *If I cut it off, I could compete in the paralympics. I'll bring it up with Coach.*

"How's your arm doing, Hope? I scheduled your appointment for tomorrow. Is 4:30 good?" Her mother asked, picking up on the disappointed worry Hope directed at her

8

splint, an omen of the imminent swim layup. Hope was surprised she'd let it slip. Of all of the people she compromised her emotions for, her mother was the only person she did it for willingly. "But I have a swim meet at 5."

"Hope, you probably won't be able to swim this season." Her mother was right, but she wasn't ready to give up on it. "You really think so?" She tried to sound unconvinced herself, but the dread of not being able to swim for months had already set in, cozying up to the discontentment and anxiety. "Yes, Hope. Although now that you can't swim, you do have time to focus on getting your grades up in your classes." Hope vaguely considered a pointed response, but she busied herself with assembling her school bag. "You have to take advantage of your opportunities." Her mother continued. "Otherwise you're not going to have many options when you have to apply next year. You're the only one responsible for your future." she said. As Hope went through the motions of her routine, it became increasingly obvious how much of a pain in the butt her arm was going to be. Dread, discontentment and anxiety got to know each other very well. The air felt uncomfortably thick as she left, and she wondered if the only time she felt capable of action was in a pool.

CHAPTER 2:
You Can't Win

The school was big to say no less. Not like his school back in Marlyn. It was huge like a castle of sorts with big walls that surrounded it. Not to mention that he could swear on all of his D.C comics that he saw a pound when walking by one of the windows. They would never have that in Myrlin he was sure. He might text Liam and Elijah the next time he gets his computer back. They would be star struck.

Seth continued to walk down the halls of his new school in a hurry. He was late, extremely late. He bets that the school announcements were halfway down by now. He knew he should have just agreed with his parents this morning. There was no point in arguing with them when they already started. But still he didn't want to change his outfit. This was a new semester and he wanted to try to look his best so he picked out his hot pink jeans with a green shirt and white tennis shoes. Seth had to say he looked pretty good no matter what his parents say.

He waved off his thoughts before looking back at the schedule the women in the front desk gave him. He had to take one more left and two right before he would make it to the auditorium. He could probably make it there in three minutes if he ran, so that's what he did.

The sound of his footsteps ranged around the halls. Seth swivelled around sharp corners as he tried to make it to the school announcement. It was better to be there than to not show up at all. He saw the wooden door at the end of the hall just as he was hitting his second right turn. Seth stopped in front of the door taking in a few breaths before opening the door.

Right away he knew it was a bad idea. All eyes were on him, students in the chairs, teachers near the walls, and the principal with a brunette girl on stage, they were all looking at him. 'Maybe it would have been better if he had just been late' he thought.

He looked through the rows of chairs before seeing an empty seat. He started to walk over to the seat before he felt the weight of his body pluminting at a rapid rate. His face hit the floor with a loud thud. Splintering pain starts to form near his nose. He got up from his spot before giving a quick glare to one of the rows behind him. He sat down at the seat letting all of the chatter filter to the background only paying attention to the people on the stage.

The rest of the announcement went by quickly. He caught sight of a few people looking and giggling at him but he was pretty much used to it by now so he didn't mind.

"I hope we all have a great rest of the year, and for future references I hope that we can all arrive at our classes in a timely manner as well".

Seth slowly sunk into the chair he was sitting in. He heard the laughter that went through the auditorium and he felt the eyes that burned holes into the back of his head. He docked his head trying to hide away from all of the staring. If he didn't see them then neither could they. Simple strategy with a simple outcome. Oh please let it be a simple outcome of laughter and teasing.

Seth followed the line of students walking out of the room. People shoved him around as they tried to get out of the auditoume quickly and meet up with their friends. He saw the brunette girl again running towards another group of students. Knowing that he was paying a bit more attention she looked really cool. Her hair was braided down and she had a purple cast on her arm that was signed with multiple names on it. Wow, he wonders what happened to her.

Before he could think anymore of it he felt someone shove him down to the floor. The aching pain of his nose doubled instantly. He quickly got up his hands quickly cupping his bloody nose.

It hurt.

He looked up to see three girls hovering over him. One was giving him a devilish smirk while the others were practically bending over laughing. What was this middle school? Were they really bullying him right now? It didn't make sense.

His thoughts probably made their way to his face since the first one, probably the leader to be honest, quirked his eyebrow up.

"What made you seem confused, princess, what's wrong?" Princess, was that supposed to be an insult? Also what does she mean 'What is the problem?'

"You pushed me, that's the problem."

The girl shook her head in dismay as Seth got up. "No, I'm sure I would know about the trip We all saw."

He saw the other two nodding. Seth shook his head in annoyance. He was starting to get irritated.

"No you pushed m-" He felt his body falling again. The pain is now forming near his but.

"No I'm sure that you tripped" With that they left him alone in the empty halls of his new school.

This was going to be so fun.

"Morning." Hope says to her friend on a Tuesday morning at school.

"Morning!" Her friend says, walking into the classroom. Wooden desks sit all around the room and math facts written on paper are taped up all around the room. A boy sits sadly at a desk.

"Get to your desks, children!" A woman with brown hair pulled up in a bun says.

Hope sits down at a random desk. It is next to the boy who is sitting sadly. He was wearing an old brown looking shirt and pants.

"Here is your homework assignment. Do it. Today."

Later, Hope sees the boy she sat next to in class getting bullied by her friend Zara. Hope wants to do something... but is worried it will affect her friendship. So Hope ignored it and walked home by herself. Hope got home, and did her homework. She sat on her pink soft bed, and slowly closed her eyes.

She was woken by someone calling "Dinner! Hope Dinner!" The voice was raspy, and not too loud, but woke Hope right up.

Hope noticed she had been asleep for a long time.

Then, she felt something pinching her. It was Hope's brother.

"Wake up! Wake up!" he said.

"I might have to pour water on you if you don't get up!"

"I am awake. Is it morning?" Hope asked.

"No, No, it's time for dinner."

Hope walked down stairs. She looked out her window. She saw the boy that her friend was bullying sitting outside.

Hope just sat down at the dining room table. She put her head down.

Chapter 3:
Seth's Parents

Seth sat in the back of the bus, thinking about how his first day had been. Bullies, a butt ton of homework, and unwavering expectations about what he should and should not do/be. It was a nightmare. But it was an escape from home for six hours of the day, so that was something. On the bright side, both his guide around the school and the teachers were pretty understanding and kind. Of his home life (or as much as he told them, they didn't need to know everything), his academic life, everything. And then there was that Hope girl.

He heard about her everywhere, and he wasn't quite sure what to make of her. She seemed kind enough, but the kindest people usually tended to be the cruelest, and it wasn't like she would ever notice him anyway. And yet, he couldn't get her off his mind. She was the captain of the swim club, an open astronomer who would be willing to give lessons to anyone who asked, and the president of the student body. She seemed to have her life all figured out. But there was a small part of him that saw through that. The way she glanced uneasily around corners, the way she rubbed her arm around her "friends" and always seemed to smile a little bit brighter when they weren't there. The way she wasn't even confident enough to help him when he was getting bullied, **and just went along with the rest of the crowd, giving him a disgusted look...MAYBE she wasn't confident at all!** The voice said, **It's all just a trick-**

He stopped himself. It wasn't worth his time to think about her and her perfect life. She wouldn't make his life any better. He would. All on his own. Then he supposed everyone would see who was giving pitied glances to who. He would show everyone! His parents, his bullies, they'd all see!

He stopped his thinking to stop a tear from rolling down his cheek, only to see the bus driver giving him a twisted grin. She'd been here since the school's opening, so, as she said, "she'd seen everything." though she still looked slightly amused.

"Alright runt. It's your stop, so get off and keep your miserable life out of my bus."
He would have laughed at the irony, but instead he just sighed.
You don't know the half of it...

***

Seth slowly rises from his ragged bedsheets and thin pillow and takes in the small dark dingy room that he now owned for the past week.He turns to look at the window that was covered by flimsy black drapes which did nothing to block the sun's angry rays of light.

Thinking dark thoughts that any boy his age shouldn't be thinking but he was, why was he hated by everyone even his own mother couldn't stand the sight of him not to me- he was broken out of his thoughts by a yell.

"BOY GET DOWN HERE!" Seth's Mother says,Seth walks calmly down the stairs and sees his mother with her usual grimace she say,

"Have you become so incompetent that you don't know how to walk down the stairs?!" she proclaimed.

His Mother watched to see if he would flinch at the harsh words like he usually did when he didn't it made her irritated.

"Your fathers at work working off the debt and I have a new gossip group to go to you're going to have to walk to school."

while she was speaking she was grabbing her bag and getting ready to leave but

Seth replied "Isn't the school 6 miles away?"

Mother says, "Maybe if you keep at it you'll lose that scrawny body of yours"

Seth slowly starts to raise his voice from the anger he was feeling while he is speaking

"That's Not Fair! You're just as skinny as I am!"

Seth's mother slowly walks toward Seth with her hand above her head,

"SLAP!!"

Seth hits the ground and slowly looks up and sees his mother's eyes that had pure unadulterated rage in them,

"DO NOT EVER SPEAK BACK TO ME BOY!!!"

Seth pushes her back and runs out of the apartment hearing his mothers yells of outrage as he runs not noticing the neighbor watching Seth with the door agape.

Chapter 4:
The Girl in the Purple Cast

    Hope comes back home from the hospital with her doctor telling her that her injury is very severe and that she will not be able to swim for months. Swimming is something Hope put a lot of time into, it was this that was going to get her into college. Meaning that when it comes time for the college scouts to come around to see her swim she won't be able to. Hope is devastated not knowing what to do. She spent the majority of her time on swimming thinking that will get her the full ride into college but without the cushion and support she had she doesn't know what to do. Her grades weren't awful but she also felt like she needed more to get her into a great college. Her parents thought very highly of hope and looked up to her to design a great future.So without the support of swimming she knew she needed to make a change. She spoke to the college coordinator at school that helps arrange the best options for the students, but she said without swimming and her grades just ok hope needed to do something to build a better application. Hope thought to herself even though her mother deeply wanted her to go to college she really needed to think about what she wanted. She decided she wanted structure and that is what a good college would give her.

Hope started researching things that are important on an application which were grades and extracurricular activities. So Hope went around to all her teachers asking what assignments were the most important and what assignments could lead to the best grades to get her into the amazing colleges she decided that she wanted.

Next Hope needed to find some activities that didn't require her to be as active because of her injury. She decided to join some clubs that would look good on a college application. The clubs she chose were the robotics club and the chess club. These activities weren't her cup of tea but they would still look excellent on an application. She didn't know how to feel about all these new people that were mentally different compared to the way she thought things work. Hope started watching videos on how to play the game of chess and ended up becoming quite good at it. In the robotics club she picked much of it up quickly once she put the negative thoughts aside, she began to have fun and enjoy it. She ended up liking these activities and being around these new people, they didn't look at her as the popular person that was the captain of the swim team. That was an image that most saw her as but in these clubs she could express herself and be something different. Hope ended up learning a lesson after joining and settling into these clubs. She went in with a negative mindset yet she realized once she stopped focusing on how her injury is not the greatest she focused on what good could have come. Since she did that she ended up finding this different side of her and a new mindset of how she looked at things!

Hope looks at her grade and suddenly feels a shock wave move throughout her whole body. Her hands begin to sweat and her heart begins to beat fast without any blood. Her feet feel like they are no longer touching the floor. She starts to feel like she can no longer breathe. She starts to gasp for air, but she can't. Her lungs felt like the Sahara desert. She looked around the classroom to see if anyone could help her. She locks eyes with Seth. She looks at him with desperation in her eyes. He can see right through her, and he knows something is wrong.

Seth helps Hope out of her chair and into the hall. He also grabs her water bottle. "It's ok, It's ok" Seth says to try and calm her down. She still can not feel her feet on the ground. His shaky hands finally opened her water bottle after a couple failed attempts. He slowly passed her the bottle. She tries to take a sip but her dry lips can't wrap around the mouth of the bottle that seemed to go on for miles. Seth is clueless on what to do. She just can't help her because he doesn't know what to do.

He sits down and leans his head on a locker and pats the floor next to him. "Come Sit" He says. Hope walks over to him, but feels like she is floating on all her grades. She slowly bends down and stretches out her long, thin legs in front of her. She starts to calm down and slowly grapes her breath and reels it back in. She lets out a big sigh and thanks him. His heart is now the one that is racing a hundred miles. He quickly regather himself and said "No problem" HE feels like he had just won the olympics. She reaches for her water bottle and takes a long big drink. She sighs again. "So, what happened there?" Seth asked "Umm every since the accident, my grade have not been as good as I want them to be and I kinda got nervous because I don't think I will be able to get into my dream school, and I will be stuck her forever" she says in a slow raspy voice "Well, I guess we will be stuck her together" He responses "Umm ok" she said in a long wired out voice. Seth quickly gathers himself up and gets up to his feet. He reaches his hand down to help Hope up. Her hand then falls into his.

Now that she'd calmed down, she attempted to wrap her head around what just happened. Why did this random new kid help her? She barely even knew Seth. She then started to feel a bit guilty. Earlier when she saw being bullied, she didn't do anything. Behind the guilt, she felt grateful for

Seth. If Seth wasn't there, what would've happened? She started to think about how to repay the favor.

"Sorry that was so embarrassing, I swear, I don't usually introduce myself like that. I'm Hope," she said as she wiped the salty tears off her flawless skin and looked down at her Red Hot Chili Peppers shirt that was slightly dampened by her tears.

"It's chill - I'm Seth, by the way," Seth tried to sound non-sholant but internally, his heart was beating faster than the amount of likes on a trendy Instagram post. They stood there just for a moment looking at each other.

Seth picked up his worn-down backpack but before he could begin to walk away Hope blurted out, "So, my friend is having a pretty laid-back thing on Friday, do you want to come?"

Did Seth just get invited to his first high school party? There's absolutely no way. She must be pranking him. Just to make sure she was being serious Seth said "so like a-a party?"

"Yeah, here's the address - my friend Zara's hosting," Hope passed him a perfectly folded note card then turned away. Seth stared as she strolled down the hallway while her shiny, dark brown braid waved perfectly from left to right.

What. Just. Happened. Every bad thing that had just happened to Seth today felt like ages ago. He knew that despite the whole "popular" image, Hope was a kind, compassionate person. He began to have this weird feeling that their little interaction today was just the start of something. He wasn't the only person feeling this way. When Hope was conversing with Seth, she felt safe and calm. Oh wait, what will Hope's friends think about her inviting some freshman newbie. Just another thing to add onto her already overfilled plate of worry.

Chapter 5:
Nightmare Party

They didn't want him to go. Figures that now that he made one friend, they all of a sudden "care about his well being." Lies. That's what it was. Lies and abusing their power over him. And it was torture. He had been so excited when he came home from school, naively assuming that they wouldn't care. BUT NOPE! Every time they saw him remotely happy, they had to come in and ruin everything.

He stared hopelessly out the window, hearing the sounds of crickets start to chirp. Usually, it would be the only thing to put him to sleep, but tonight it felt just as awful as everything else. He looked at the watch on his wrist, which he hadn't bothered to take off after his argument with his parents. The party started in ten minutes. The place was only a few minutes walk away, and if he listened closely, he swore he could hear the sounds of it getting started. If

only he could be there. He saw his raggedy curtains sway-
ing in the outside breeze, and the air was quickly pushed
through the open window(which his parents refused to
close because of "Reasons"), making his room feel even
more lifeless. That's when it hit him. The open window.

His window wasn't too far from ground level, so he
wasn't likely to break anything if he went out that way.
And with the TV blaring in the other room, there was no
way they'd notice. There was still a question of how he'd
get back in when he got home, but he could think about
that when it was important. He didn't have time for hesitation. He sat up from his sideways position on his bed,
un-crinkled his outfit that had cost him all his saved money,
and carefully approached the window, cringing at every
squeak in the floorboards. After what felt like an eternity
of walking, he made it three feet away from his bed, where
his window hung open invitingly. He summoned all his
courage, and stretched one leg through the window. Then
the other. All of a sudden, his legs were dangling through
the air, and there was no turning back. It was amazing. He
tucked his legs in so they were touching the outer walls,
pushed his hands forward, and let go.

He didn't quite know how he managed it, but he made
it safely to the ground. His grey shirt now looked kind of
disgusting, but what did he care? He had never felt more
free. He ran down the driveway and did a little happy spin.
He started walking towards the address tucked safely in
his pocket, but before he left, he spared one last glance

over his shoulder. He decided right then and there that he never wanted to come back to that god forsaken apartment. He pondered for a moment where he could go, but nothing came up. Perhaps he could talk to Hope about it. She seemed understanding enough, and definitely had connections. But either way, it didn't matter right now. He had a friend who cared, and as he walked away from his old life, hands in his pockets, the whole world seemed to move with him.

The house was huge, and as he walked confidently towards it, he felt his doubt setting in. *Maybe this wasn't a good idea. . .* he shook that thought out of his head. He'd be fine, as long as he kept his chin down and hung with Hope. Which wouldn't be too difficult. He knocked on the giant victorian knocker, and waited for someone to let him in. as he rocked on his heels impatiently, he looked through the windows. Blaring pink-orange lights stung his eyes and lit up the room. Music blasted through the windows, threatening to burst his eardrums. People were whispering and chatting in cliques, and a few noticed him staring and looked weirded out. It was still awesome. It felt like a fresh start. The door swung open, and he nearly squealed in excitement that he got to actually go inside.

"**WHAT are you doing here NERD?!**" the person who opened the door squawked as all color drained from Seth's face.

The ring leader bully from school, Zara, was menacingly towering over him, and giving him a look that shouldn't even be given to mosquitos. Seth gulped and held still, preparing for a punch in the gut, but nothing came. He squeezed his eyes open, only to see the bully still staring. She kind of just looked confused. Seth didn't particularly have the energy to do another crazy/brave (depending on how you looked at it) thing tonight, but it seemed like he had to. So he swallowed his fear, and tried to speak calmly in a shaking voice.

"I-I-I um...HOPE INVITED ME!" he finally blurted.

"Yeah, that's **LIKELY!**" she said sarcastically. Seth was feeling a bit angry. Where was Hope? Couldn't she save HIM for once? No one ever seemed to be around when he needed it... **NO ONE EVEN WANTS ME-**

"Seth?"

A voice cut through the tension and darkness, breaking Seth out of his spiral. He spun around to see Hope in a long sea green and gold dress, looking uncomfortable.

"FINALLY!" the bully exclaimed, "**Hope, this weirdo thinks you invited him! Wanna sort this out?**"

Seth looked pleadingly at the girl he barely knew, and Hope gave him a slight smile.

"He's with me, **Zara.**"

Seth was about to celebrate internally when he realized what had been said. THIS was ZARA?! Hope invited him to a party hosted by the person who hated him most... **IS THIS SOME SORT OF ATTEMPT AT A CRUEL JOKE-**

Seth stopped, aware of Hope's eyes burning into the back of his head as she approached from behind. He breathed in for four beats, out for six. Once, twice, until he was calm. He looked up and met Zara's eyes.

"Hey, I'm Seth," he said, extending his hand, "Nice to meet you **ZARA.**"

The girl just let out an evil chuckle, waved him off, and opened the door wider. Hope rushed to Seth's side, squeezed his hand reassuringly, and led him inside the huge home.

"Why are you upset?" She said.
Seth didn't respond. "I said, WHY ARE YOU UPSET!?"
Hope yelled that so a lot of people at the party started staring at her.
"I'm sorry. I'm sorry. I mean, I invited you to this party and you seem... uncomfortable." Hope said.
"I'm just a little... tense." Seth said.
"I don't get it." Hope said.

"I don't get why you would." Seth said, rolling his eyes. Seth walked away quickly.

"Seth, come back!" Hope said, chasing after Seth, but he disappeared in the crowd.

As Seth tries to find a place to sit down because he feels a little on edge with people constantly encouraging him to drink. While running around frantically to find a place to sit and calm down he ends up knocking the punch bowl all over him. This causes his bully Zara to make another one of her many snarky comments. Zara ends up getting all her friends to humiliate Seth. Seth feels so terrible it causes him to unleash a deep rage and anger that Seth has never shown before. He saw his new friend Hope standing by her friends and not saying anything to defend him. Suddenly in that moment with all eyes on him, he began to think about what has come of his life. His mom practically thinks of him as a scrawny kid who she doesn't care about. And his new friend Hope, who Seth thought was nice has turned against him. At that moment Seth felt like a total zero. He has felt bad at times but never as low as this. He didn't know how to process this so he decided to stay quiet and keep his head down. All that Seth wanted to come of this party is to have fun and hang out with the somewhat popular kids. He thought that a popular girl like Hope doesn't invite a guy like Seth to a big party everyday. But boy was he wrong he ended up making a fool of himself and feeling like someone that doesn't matter.

"Hey everyone, just to let you know, the party is continuing outside in the pool. Don't miss out"

It seemed like Zara was addressing her. Of course she was going to miss out! I mean, Her left arm was absolutely useless in this cast. She watched everyone hustle outside as the pool filled up. It was a wild party, so maybe if she could swim, she wouldn't have as much fun as in her swimming lessons. Hope headed over to grab a glass of punch to sooth the dryness in her throat, but she remembered Seth had spilled it all out. She got some grape juice instead. She was afraid to admit it, but without being able to push herself forward one stroke at a time leaving all the depressing emotions behind with the pushed back water, she just wanted to weep it out. But she didn't want to show how weak and helpless she could actually be because she had already worked up a strong trusting reputation. Hope started to pour the thick purple liquid into a plastic cup when she noticed that same boy who helped her out in her panic attack, his hands fumbling on his grey V neck shirt. She noticed that the punch stain from earlier still hadn't dried.

"Can I join you?"

"Fine." He muttered under his breath. Hope walked up to him with two grape juice filled cups, careful to avoid the empty glasses and food bits on the floor.

"Why don't we go sit outside and breathe some fresh air?"

"Sure." Seth agreed. So the two high schoolers silently trudged outside to find a private place where they could sit and talk. They found one spot which was shaded by a thick hedge and seemed designed just for them.

"So, how's it going?" She asked, hoping for a taste of conversation.

"HOW'S IT GOING? YOU MEAN AFTER I MAKE A FOOL OF MYSELF IN FRONT OF EVERYONE, RUIN MY BEST AND ONLY GOOD SHIRT, GET BULLIED AGAIN BY YOUR STUPID FRIENDS, AND FINALLY AFTER YOU BETRAYED ME BY LETTING YOUR FRIEND GETTING BULLIED AND LEAVING IT TO ME TO DEAL WITH? YOU MEAN AFTER THAT?"

"NO! I didn't want any of that to happen!" She replied in a pleading voice

"THEN WHY DID YOU ACT LIKE I DIDN'T EVEN EXIST BACK THERE?"

"You don't understand Seth! Then they'll bully me too and I'll have no one to talk to! It will also ruin my reputation!" She was on the verge of tears now and grasped her knees for comfort.

"YOU CARE ABOUT YOUR REPUTATION RIGHT NOW?!"

"YES! Because you've never had one to understand!" The impact of these words hit him like a painful bullet and it took a long time for them to sink in. They continued to glare into each others faces until Seth spoke up,

"Well... OF COURSE YOU WOULDN'T CARE! YOUR TOO COWARDLY TO STAND UP TO ANYONE ANYWAYS."

"You don't know what I'M going through do you?"

"NO! What are you going through then, lack of friends?" He laughed at his own joke then paused to give Hope a chance to continue.

"No. After I broke my arm-"

"You experienced a lot of pain, right. I also experience pain, but in a different way."

"YOU NEVER LISTEN!"

"Fine then"

"Anyways, after I broke my arm, I had nothing to do. Swimming was my life, and now, well, I guess you can say I feel tormented." Hope paused, expecting for Seth to say something, but all he did was clutch his cup tightly in between his knees and stared into the remaining dregs of it. So she continued

"Anyways, now because my life has been snatched away from me I guess I haven't been myself lately."

"Well, while you're deciding what to do with your life, I'm getting bullied nonstop with no one to go to. My parents will probably ground me for months after what I did. So because i'm not worth anything here, all there is to do left is run away.

"NO, Seth NOOO!"

But he had already given one last look at Hope's tear splattered face, then turned his back on her and disappeared into the pitch black sky.

Chapter 6:
In Full Color

After the party Seth had a chance to cool off. As he walked into school with a better mindset to hopefully make up with Hope. He thought that Hope might have seen clearly on how she shouldn't hang out with her jerks of friends. But as he walked in the door he stood there for a second pinching himself to make sure what he was seeing was real. He saw Hope talking and laughing with those "great" friends that humiliated him. He thought she was going to change but he was wrong. That deep rage came up from deep inside and revisited him once again and he stormed off. Hope saw him as he ran off and she felt ashamed of herself to do that to Seth again. At that moment Seth felt a need for justice for himself. He thought running away was the best option, but he decided not to yet and see how things play out the rest of the day.

Zara laughed Heartily at Hope's joke, and Hope smiled uncomfortably. The party that felt like an eternity ago was still on her mind. More specifically, one person. Seth. She wasn't sure what to do about him. She was angry with him, sure. Livid, even! He had left with no warning, acting like he was the most important thing in the world, and like he was so weak he couldn't take some punches without breaking.

But on the other hand, maybe he really couldn't. A small part of her was actually worried about him. He did say he was gonna run away, and she didn't want that for him. Increasing her worry even more, she hadn't seen Seth for the past few days, and no signs of him this morning either. She couldn't even check on him! It's not like she knew where he lived!

Suddenly, she felt a gaze on her back, and she spun around to see him standing there. He tensed, then turned and quickly disappeared into the flood of students. She shouted after him, not registering the weird looks she was getting, then she quickly stopped when she felt a cold hand on her shoulder.

"Dude, What is up with you today?" Zara said in a fake concerned voice.

Shrugging off her grip she panickingly said, "oh, it's nothing at all really, just a stupid-"

"It's not that weird kid from the party, is it?" she said, her dark eyes staring into Hope's soul, "He was an idiot alright. Made for some good laughs though."

Before she could register that words were coming out of her mouth, she had already finished her sentence

"He's not that bad Zara. I-I mean, he's not great, but he's kinda cool."

"What is he, your boyfriend or something?" Zara said coldly.

"WHAT?! Of course not!" she said, grossed out, "Look, I'm coming over to your house later, can we talk then?"

"I guess," Zara mumbled, "but why not now?"

"We have a weird art class shoved in the day to intro-duce a buddy grade project, and I had to be there 2 minutes ago. See you later!" she explained quickly before running down the hallway.

As she left, she saw someone rush up to Zara and say something to the effect of: "We need to talk! I've got new information on..." she thought the conversation was then drowned out by the noise of the hallway, but she couldn't shake the uneasy feeling that the conversation was put on hold because they'd seen her. She pushed her curiosity aside and made her way down the hallways to the assigned classroom. It was a new direction for her and she hoped she was going the right way.

Hope was surprised when she saw Seth for the second time that morning, going down the same hallway she was. She thought about going up and talking, but she was late, and still upset. Then they both went down the same hallway again. And again...and..again. She was getting uncomfortable all over again now, and when Seth stopped at the same door as her, the overwhelming urge to run away kicked in, and she almost listened to it.

"What are you doing here?" Seth asked cynically

"I could ask the same question." Hope said sarcastically, standing her ground.

"Um, this is my art class!" they said simultaneously.

Seth stared at her for a second, then opened the door and bolted into the classroom right before everyone else poured in. Hope struggled to find her way through the chaos, and eventually made it, only to see every other table already had two people at it, and the one person without a buddy...

JUST MY LUCK...

She sat down at Seth's table and they both stared ahead at nothing in particular. She felt like everyone's eyes were burning into her head. How would she ever build her reputation back up after this? A lot of hiding things, that was for sure. She sighed and pulled her sketchbook out of her bag, only to see Seth already starting to draw in his. She stole a glance at his page and was shocked at what she saw. Even his sketches were so realistic she had to do a double take. She'd known he was good at art for a while now, but as he flipped through to find a blank page to work on, she saw pages and pages of diagrams, landscapes, portraits, and entire maps of fake worlds, all labeled and planned out perfectly. She also saw a lot of abstract pieces flying by. Zigzags and sharp colors were everywhere, and one look at the dates on those pages told her he had been working on these outside of school, which was against the rules. But who was she to say that? They were beautiful!

"Wow..." she murmured as the teacher walked in.

"Alright everyone! Let's get today started!" the teacher said, with her usual exclamations. She then turned around and wrote the worst thing Hope could've ever imagined on the whiteboard.

Buddy project: Self expression!
Show who you truly are in art!

At that moment, all Hope wanted to do was curl up in a ball and go home.

OH GOSH. . .

But her thoughts were interrupted when the teacher came around handing out four pieces of paper stapled together, dropping them on everyone's desks. Her heart skipped a beat as she stared into the art project instruction page. The teacher had talked about the project in class before, warning it was coming up, but it seemed unreal then. But with the tiny back letters printed on this blank white paper, she was going to have to take it as permanent. She looked up at that lonely boy with the green glasses and sighed.

"Oh well. It's too late to change partners now." Hope felt a new kind of awkwardness around Seth because of the big fight, but she was still too mad at Seth's arrogance to forgive him. So she heaved her heavy backpack over her shoulder and apprehensively walked over to his desk. He was too busy burying himself in the 4 page booklet the teacher handed out to them before, to notice Hope until she was basically standing right behind him.

"Could I have a seat?"

"Well you have no choice, do you?"

"Whatever, so how do you put self expression into art anyways?" Hope asked, flicking her brunette ponytail out of the way and pulling in a chair.

"Well, how do you usually feel on a daily basis?" Seth asked with a bored expression on his face and resting his chin on his left hand.

"Me? Well, I have a strong longing to swim, especially in this heat. That's one. And I also feel really stressed because of all the homework we're receiving and again not being able to swim. That makes two. So, What about you?" Seth's freckle covered face turned a blazing vibrant red and it was hard to decide if his hair was a better colour then his face.

"Well.. I... ugh... feel really angry." The last three words were barely audible and Hope had to strain her ears to hear them."

"At who? Oh... Ya. Zara." The next few moments between them were blank silence and you could hear a pin drop.

"So," Seth finally spoke. "Maybe to express my rage, we could sculpt a flaming fireball shooting towards a cowering figure with their arms over their head to express your stress. Sounds good?"

"Wow! How do you think of such good ideas in such a short period of time?"

"Practise I guess. Anyways this is what I was thinking." Seth pulled out a blank notebook and flipped the pages until he was satisfied.

"Ahh, here it is." Seth showed Hope a carefully drawn labeled diagram of a clay sculpture kneeling with their arms thrown over their head. In the distance you could plainly see a brown circular rock with raging fire propelling it. It was beautiful. But before Hope could reply, Seth had shut the notebook, tucked it in his backpack, grabbed a stack of books, and rushed away.

Out of anyone, ANYONE! Why did he have to get paired up with Hope? The girl who refused to stand up to her fake friend. Of course! Why didn't he think of it before? She was using him, using him to get more popularity because that's all she cared about. Friends. Reputation. Popularity. Good grades. Maybe he didn't get paired up with Hope coincidentally, maybe that day when he dropped his art notebook and Hope caught a glance of it, she knew how good he was at art and asked the teacher for him as a partner.

"Look everyone! Time for a little fun! Princess come here!" Came the high pitched squeal of Zara. There was a boys bathroom up ahead, if he could just reach the stall...

"Got you!" Sure enough, he was dangling upside down in the air as Zara's firm grip held his left foot tightly. He had darted in the direction of the boys washroom only to be scooped up by another member of Zara's gang Victoria Wellson and passed on to Zara herself. His glasses had crashed to the ground and cracked and he was certain his parents weren't going to buy him new ones.

"Seth, Seth, Seth. What a mess you are. It wouldn't make any difference if we messed you up some more. Your life is already a dump yard. Merssia, will you do the honors?"

"Sure. Stop squirming you little baby." Merrisa appeared, tossing her sleek wavy brown hair over her shoulders and preparing her perfectly tanned fist into a ball and kissing it with her red lipstick coated lips.

"Come on Marr! Make this quick. If I don't get enough time to apply my makeup, I'll die."

44

"Chill down Vicky! You'll have 10 minutes to do it, and if that's not enough then say Seth Pushed you and gave you a nosebleed. Like, this." Before he could react, he experienced blinding pain. It was like Merrisa's fist was the brown rock and she transported the fire onto his nose. He pushed his free hand to stop the steady stream of blood which had already stained his green cargo camouflage pants.

"Ready for another one?" No! No! Please No! Cried the voice inside his head. He tried screaming, for a teacher or something. But it was almost like he had swallowed his voice, nothing came out. The flaming fist was approaching, closer and closer, and...

"STOP!" Merrisa moved, and he could see what the distraction was. A girl with a short ponytail and a light denim jacket covering a black and white striped T-shirt stood with blazing fury, her hands holding the shape of fists. The tight black leggings led to her teal Vans hiding white ankle socks, her legs wide apart.

"STOP!" She screamed again

"Hope, you know we're just having a little fun here."

"FUN? WHAT DID SETH EVER DO TO YOU?"

"Look Hope. I didn't get revenge for that time he talked back to me. It was so rude." Merrisa snarled.

"THAT WAS BECAUSE YOU WERE WEARING THAT DUMB CROWN ON YOUR HEAD!"

"I was wearing the crown because Zara gave it to me for my sweet sixteen. It was made out of solid gold. Too bad it was borrowed as it wasn't on sale." Merrisa sighed

"WELL, THAT DOESN'T MEAN YOU CAN PUNCH HIM! YOU CALL HIM PRINCESS ALL THE TIME AND HE DOESN'T PUNCH YOU!"

"Look, that's because he is one, or at least he wants to be one. Didn't you hear the story of him wearing pink dresses and shirts saying stuff like 'bow to the queen' when he was little. Zara smirked.

"How did you-?"

"I have my ways Seth. Anyways gang, let's go." As Zara dropped Seth to the floor, Hope turned on her heel and scampered in the opposite direction, her ponytail swinging side to side.

He had almost made it to history when Seth heard muffled cries coming from the girls washroom. Before he had time to question who it could be, straight black hair came into view which could only belong to Zara. She had her arm around a girl with puffy red eyes and a light denim jacket. There were still tears running down her kind face.

"Don't worry Hope. You'll get to punch Seth next time." Before he could eavesdrop anymore, the history teacher steered him into the classroom leaving him to ponder on his own.

Chapter 7:
Making Sacrifices

Two days later, Seth stood in the hallway, barely noticing the bell ringing. Everything since he started here felt like a blur, and nothing felt real anymore. Up felt like down, light felt dark, no one could be trusted, and nothing was sacred. Basically, it felt a little worse than normal. **Yeah, something tells me that's probably not good...**

He hadn't even felt like getting out of bed yesterday. He wasn't sad or happy per say, just kind of thoughtful and tired. He hadn't had much energy to draw or do anything productive, so he just kind of stared out his window. That day they were off school, so he could technically do nothing, and for the first time in a long time, his parents made it so he actually didn't. Which was odd. Usually he had to cook and clean everything for them. **Maybe after grounding me, they forgot that I even exist...**

Everything was crashing into each other in his head that day (and still kind of was). Mostly contradicting thoughts about Hope. She wasn't a good friend, but maybe he wasn't either? They both hadn't really had much experience in that department. She cared about her reputation way too much in his opinion, but she seemed like she'd sacrificed a lot to get there, plus she had just almost given it all away, just for him. She still kind of seemed like she hung out with the bullies, but it almost seemed like she couldn't get away, and boy did he know what that was like. So it might have been against his better judgement, and you would never hear him say it, but...he cared about her.

Still, he had some control over this mess. All of his homework was done, including the first draft of his art project with Hope, which he had already had mostly done, but added a few details to this morning. They only had to turn in a rough draft thus far, but since he had started drawing this design way before the project was announced, he was almost on his final step of the drawing phase. The art teacher had been very impressed by his art this year, and he did not intend to break that pattern.

The only thing he had to worry about was Hope's part. She was in charge of choosing the color palette (and eventually doing a lot of the actual sculpting), and since they basically had not communicated at all, he wasn't sure if she even did it or not. But she got decent grades, and that couldn't have come from nothing.

Finally breaking out of his race car of thought, Seth casually noticed that he was supposed to be in art class TEN MINUTES AGO. so he smiled tightly and casually walked ONE HUNDRED MILES PER HOUR DOWN THE HALLWAY.

When he got to art, he was surprised to see Hope wasn't there yet either. Neither were the few Zara followers that were in this class. It had to just be a coincidence, right? He shuffled across the room to his seat awkwardly, and waited to be called on to turn in his project. Ten minutes later, Seth's group was being called up, and Hope still wasn't there. The teacher skimmed his drawing and looked up at him.

"Where's the color palette?" she asked patiently.

"oh-I-" he stuttered, "Hope was supposed to do that."

"And where is she?" the teacher asked, "Seth, you know I can't accept this without the color palette."

"I...don't know," he said quickly, "Look, if I see her I'll tell her, could you just look at the drawing, I mean I think it's a pretty important part-"

The teacher quieted him, looked the drawing over more intently, and looked up after a while, stunned.

"This is incredible, Seth!" she said, "it would make a great entry into-" she stopped herself and chuckled.

"Would make a great entry into...what?" Seth asked, hearing whispers already emerging from the rest of the class.

The art teacher just smiled mischievously and said, "Don't worry about it. You'll all find out tomorrow."

The class erupted in whispers, rumors, guessing, obnoxious interrogation, and face palming. Seth went back to his seat, layed his head on his desk, and hoped that Hope would get there soon.

Hope had missed the entirety of art class, so Seth had rightfully assumed that she wasn't at school. So then it also seemed fair that when he saw her in the hallway at his lunch time, that he got a little snippy.

Seth had never liked cafeterias, with their cliques and smells, so he tended to eat outside. He was (staying hidden from the rest of the people outside by hiding in a corner) doing that when Hope approached him.

"Hey Seth, can I ask you something?" her voice cut through the silent air behind him, making him jump.

"Hope?" Seth asked cynically, spinning around, "Where were you today?"

Hope rubbed her arm, looking guilty, "Sorry for ditching you like that, there were things I needed to take care of."

"Like what?"

"...Zara and her friends were trailing me" she whispered, a tear rolling down her cheek before she wiped it away.

Stunned, Seth moved closer, "What did they do to you?"

"They said some pretty messed up stuff," Hope explained quietly and... they said if I hung out with you any longer, they would hurt you again...I-I can't let them do that to you Seth. th-they-they're not my friends anymore."

Seth didn't know what to say. Hope had finally had enough, and stood up for both of them, which was great, but...

"Why would you do that?" Seth asked. The words came out harsher than intended.

"What?" Hope said, pausing her attempt to stand up and walk away.

"What?!" Seth said, "You just gave away your entire reputation for me! I can't be worth **that much.**"

"Of course you are!" Hope exclaimed, "You matter to me Seth! And it already happened anyway, so there's no point debating it now. That wasn't even what I came here to ask you."

Again, Seth was at a loss for words. He couldn't believe Zara would stoop that low, but more importantly that Hope cared. **Maybe someone does want me...** Finally he patted the spot and the ground next to him, and Hope sat down. Once Seth started talking, he could barely stop.

"Look, I might tell you what I mean later, but I'll just say this for now. I KNOW what it's like to have awful people in your life. And I don't want you getting hurt. So don't hang out with them, but if you're not supposed to hang out with me, then please don't! I don't want them to hurt you-"

"Seth!" Hope cried, "Let me make my own decisions please. You're the first person who's actually seen me for me, and I don't want to lose that. So if I say I want to hang out with you, I'm going to hang out with you. Who cares what they think or do about me!"

Hope stood up and put her hand on her hips, looking across the field at the sky. Seth stood up next to her, leagues shorter. He reached out and squeezed her hand reassuringly, like she did for him before.

"What was it you wanted to ask me?" he asked, remembering that she meant to ask something before he exploded at her.

"Oh," Hope chuckled, turning to him, "I thought that we could find a creative way to still hang out that even Zara can't complain about, and...I need a math tutor if I want to get my grades up. I've heard you've tutored before, so I figured I'd ask."

"Haha." he said, smiling, "Clever. Yeah I might just be able to help you out. ...by the way, sorry for exploding at you. Still figuring out how to be a good friend to you."

"You and me both." Hope said.

The bell rang that his lunch was over, and that Hope was probably an hour late to her class. She stood frozen there for a second, then rushed a goodbye to him and bolted into the building. Seth picked up his bag and did the same, smiling. He thought he was a decent math tutor. He was pretty monotone and serious when it came to that though, so he hoped she didn't see it differently.

I mean... how bad could it really go?

Chapter 8:
Spilled Secrets

Hope goes to her locker after the tutoring session and finds a letter in there from "Seth" telling her to come to his house with the address. She goes over there and sees how his parents treat him and then they talk about it. He tells her he wants to run away and she says she will help him, but they get caught and Seth is grounded.

Hope pushed open the heavy doors revealing a gleaming tile floor with countless lockers surrounding it. She guessed that her tutoring lesson went slightly over time as normally the school custodian would clean this area at 3:50. She walked over to her locker and grabbed her coat and fabric book bag holding all the information needed for her homework. It had been such a long day, filled with drama, headaches, and assignments bearing multiple big fat 'B's. How long until she could finally lead her own life and make choices for herself? She slammed her locker door shut, but all the force caused a sealed white envelope to flutter out. Strongly baffled by this new finding, she bent over and picked up the envelope. She ripped it open, showing a short printed letter addressed to her.

Hope,

If you can, please come over to my house at 4:15 today. I would really enjoy some company. Also, I wanted to apologize for my actions the other day. I regret them severely.

Signed, Seth

What was this? Some kind of joke? In the tutoring lesson, Seth was giving her the stink eye and ignored her as much as possible. But all the same, there was a chance that he had changed his mind completely and wanted to surprise her. She glanced at her watch and gasped. If she was going, she had about 15 minutes to get there and he lived surprisingly far away. Her slow walk broke into a fast jog as she tried her best to be on time. Her house wasn't very far from the school and she could probably get there in 3 minutes at this pace. Her throat suddenly became awfully dry and she was quite disappointed when she found out she drank all her water in chemistry. But on the bright side, she had just stopped running, and Hope stood gasping and panting on their front step, clutching a cramp on her side. A few moments later, her mom stood in the doorway with a brown braid in the back and holding a platter of cut cheese and crackers.

"You're back early! I thought you would arrive at 4:05!"

"Mom, I NEED you to drive me to this address A.S.A.P!!" Hope pleaded, showing her the letter

"Why? This is so far away!" She protested

"Just take the letter!"

"Fine, fine. Tell your brother I'm taking you to visit a friend, I'll get the car keys."

"Sure." She agreed, then shouted up the stairs

"HEY NOLAN! ME AND MOM ARE GOING OUT, BE BACK IN 20!"

"Whatever." He replied. Hope then swiftly picked out a nice blouse, some jeans, purple flats, and sprayed some of her favorite perfume so she could make a good impression. She then rushed downstairs and called dibs on shotgun, only to remember that her brother wasn't coming. Hope watched in awe as the garage door slid open on command which appeared to be hiding a blue Toyota Corolla Cross which smelled strongly of gasoline. She threw her uninjured hand to her nose and pinched, attempting to prevent any more headaches. When she threw open the passenger side door, Hope sank into the lush leather seat and asked her mom to turn on some pop music to set the vibe going.

"So, how's school been going lately honey?" Her mom asked when they set off

"The usual. Seth's still mad at me."

"You know, you really should get some different friends! I don't like Zara, Merrisa, and- what's that other girl's name?"

"Victoria." Hope corrected her "And Ava hangs out with them too. She just isn't present when the b-bullying happens." She winced at the word, as it sounded much worse when said aloud.

"Don't worry, I'm sure you're handling the situation just fine! Plus, I've talked to Charlotte Torres' mom and she sounds like a kind person to be friends with."

"Yeh, I guess so." She stared out the window resting her cheek in the palm of her hand. In the distance there was a series of gloomy grey apartment buildings, and in one of the tiny glass windows was probably Seth, sitting in his room and expecting a visitor.

Her mom pulled into the parking lot beside the apartment building and Hope started walking over to the front desk. Inside introduced a new kind of gloominess. The lobby was completely empty, and the wooden chairs stood untouched and abandoned in the waiting area. The floor was creaky and the countertops gathered lots of dust. How could Seth and his family possibly live here? They must have major financial problems, Hope guessed. She walked over to the lady standing behind the front desk and asked what if Seth Bradly stayed at this hotel. Luckily, she said he had arrived just 2 minutes ago and he stayed in room 402. She thanked the woman and went over to the elevator where she pressed the faded number four. She adjusted her handbag which held her phone, wallet, home keys, pen, and some other contents. She was nervous, and also excited to forgive him. Maybe this would be her one chance for a true friend, something she never had before. Hope stepped out of the elevator when the familiar ding sounded as it skidded to a stop at floor 4. Unfortunately, the rooms were organized in descending order so she had to walk all the way to the very end of the hallway. Because the room was an even number, it was on the side of the building which had a clear view right into another apartment building.

She knocked briskly on the wooden door and suddenly worried if her outfit was too formal for this hang out period. But when a man in a blue button up shirt appeared with black jeans, she then felt a wave of relief that she did dress up like she did. The man standing right in front of her was overweight and was in desperate need for a beard shave. He also had glasses like his son.

"Hi! I was wondering If a Seth Bradly lives here with you?"

"No Seth here, sorry." He barked back, and attempted slamming the door in her face before Hope stepped in and put her foot in the way. She was honestly about to turn around, but the woman at the front desk sounded pretty confident in the whereabouts of Seth.

"Are you sure? The woman who works here told me Seth Bradly arrived just a few minutes ago." She questioned, hands on her hips.

"Like I said, there's no Seth Bradly in this building! Now get out!" The guy was now having trouble keeping his voice down, and a few residents stuck their heads out of the door to see what was going on.

At that time, A redhead teenager walked past the doorway and after seeing the girl who was standing in the doorway, he gasped and stood there mortified.

"Boy! I said I didn't want to see your ugly face again in my sight or you'd be in big trouble! I grounded you after the party, remember?" And at that moment, the dad raised his large hand and whacked Seth in the face. Hope stood horrified in the hallway, watching him massage the hurting area on his cheek which had a purple bruise growing in place.

"Seth! You alright?" Hope pushed back the man in the hallway and rushed to his aid.

"No no I'm fine." He replied hastily

"You sure?"

"Yes! But, how on earth did you get here?"

"What do you mean? You sent me a letter!"

"Wait.. What letter?"

"You mean you didn't send me that letter?" Hope asked slowly.

"Ok little girl, this is private property and I will not tolerate you being here. GET OUT!" The forgotten father yelled.

"No dad, she's staying. I need to ask her something." Before the man could react, Seth grabbed her arm and dragged her to a small and messy bedroom at the farthest corner of the flat. She suddenly acknowledged how gross the stench was in the room, smelling like rotten food and burning cigarettes. They were finally alone when the door locked behind them and Hope at last got a chance to blurt out all her feelings that had been bubbling up inside her for the past ten minutes.

"Those are your parents?" Hope gaped at Seth

"Wish I could say no." He muttered ashamed with his eyes in his hands

"But, they're horrible people!"

"EXACTLY! THAT'S WHY I WANTED TO RUN AWAY!" He roared at her

"Oh. I thought it was because you were grounded."

"I've been grounded for the past ten years and it's always been a part of my day, I guess."

"You shouldn't have to go through this I'll-" Her voice trembled and broke and she stared at the ground with a blank expression on her face.

"Help me run away?" He pleaded

"Then hope for the best!" She locked eyes with Seth for a second, putting on a weak smile.

"Thank you. You don't know what this means to me." Seth replied, breaking the unbearable silence.

"You could... stay at my place? I'm sure my mom wouldn't mind." Hope suggested

"I dunno." He denied the offer uneasily.

"Come on. She's a lot kinder than your parents. She'll accept without hesitation, I know she will."

"Are you sure?"

"Seth, you want to run away.. Right? Well this is your one chance. You'll sneak out of the flat while I distract your parents. Then I'll say I'm heading home and take you! I'll pay for a taxi, and you'll be free in no time."

"That sounds risky... I LOVE IT!" Hope exhaled a large amount of air she had no idea she was holding.

He would finally be free!

Hope rushed out of the room and found Seth's parents who were watching TV. They were not in a good mood to talk, but desperate times called for desperate matters.

"What are you doing here?" The dad snarled, without looking her way. She froze in her tracks, then continued.

"I'm sorry to disturb you, but I just wanted to give you a heads up that your bathroom sink is not working." Hope was about to say she would be going out now, but when she saw Seth still sneakily crawling across the floor, she continued. "You should also try out a different apartment, this one-" She caught herself just in time and hastily filled in the blanks before rushing out.

"Is a bit far from the school. Well, bye!" She smiled, ignoring his glare. She quickly caught up with Seth who was waiting just outside the door.

"Well, are you ready to book the taxi?"

"Yes! This will be my first time ever riding one!"

"No it won't Seth Bradly. You're grounded." His Dad shouted from the other room.

Chapter 9:
Meeting Mrs. Volk

Seth sat in art class with his favorite teacher, Mrs. Volk. She wore ripped paint splattered jeans, a paint covered smock and a paintbrush coated with pink paint dripping onto her smock was tucked behind her ear. "Good day class!" She said. "There is an art contest soon and I strongly suggest you all enter. The winner will get to travel to Mexico and attend a month long art camp." "You should enter!" Hope said, appearing at a desk by Seth. "Like I would win." Seth said. "Well, you should at least try." Ms. Volk the art teacher said. "And that little notebook," She said, pointing to the blue notebook on his desk. "It has some good stuff." She flipped through the drawings in the notebook. Ms. Volk walked into the middle of the room and started babbling about shapes in art. But Seth was thinking about the contest. Should I enter? If I lose will Zara bully me?

As Seth comes home feeling truly excited about something for once in a long time he starts practicing and preparing for the art contest. He sorted his art supplies and began to draw and watch videos on how to improve his skills. That day his mom saw him happy and busier doing that, than the million other chores she makes him do. Seth does so many chores on a regular that it could be considered child labor. His mom starts to discourage him and tells him that his art looked as if someone had found it in a five year olds coloring book. She took all his art supplies that cost a good deal of money that he had earned for selling some of his older and more basic drawings. He had spent hours on those because it's hard to add jass to a couple of cheap pencils he "borrowed" from someone in his history class. Those drawings had taken him hours upon hours to complete and he had no time to sit there teddiesely to make more to sell. The only person he could turn to was Hope, which he had felt guilty about but, how else was he going to get the money in time to buy the new art supplies and practice with them.

✳✳✳

Seth was tired. He had woken up way earlier than any average human being ever should, just so that he could get to school early. He had thought about asking hope for help, but he already leaned on her a lot. He thought of one last person to turn to, so he was heading there now.

He fell through the school doors, and shuffled down the hallway, watching as people huddled in blankets for their before school activities. It was unnaturally cold for April, and it seemed everyone was shivering. He had made the mistake of not taking a jacket, and at this point he wouldn't have been surprised if someone pointed out that all of his limbs had frozen off. And to make it worse, it was finally getting warmer, but now it was humid. As the cherry on top, the teachers making their way through the hallways meant a lot of groaning and echoing walls, making him feel like an alien walking through hallways he'd walked in for months.

He stood before the door of the art room, everything a blurry haze. He cautiously opened the door to a confused Mrs. Volk, who gave an awkward smile.

"Seth?" she asked, "What are you doing here so early-"

She noticed the bags under his eyes, messy hair, and shivering all in one moment before saying, "here, take a seat, I'll get you a blanket."

This was one of the things he loved most about his teacher. She was like him. Constantly getting stuck in other people's problems, having to make them feel better, and not asking questions. Or so he thought, until-

"Are you alright Seth?" her voice cut in questioningly, "You look like you haven't slept in days."

"I-i'm fine," he sighed, "my house is just far away, so I had to get up early to get here early."

"Your parents won't drive you?" she half asked, looking concerned.

"N-no. Mrs. Volk, may I ask you something?" he said, smiling weakly.

"Of course, Seth," she smiled, "that's what I'm here for!"

He felt his heart beating, and felt shallow breaths coming from his lungs. Time felt like it was slowed down, and the longer he spent waiting looking at his teacher, the more awkward it would get. This was such a simple thing, so why was he so scared? Scratch that, he knew why. Everyone he'd ever cared about had hurt him, even if they didn't mean too. But he knew she wouldn't hurt him! So why were the words getting caught in his throat. Of course, he knew the answer to that too.

Because even knowing that, I still don't trust myself or them enough to feel safe...

But... she won't hurt me.

With that little conformation, he looked up and blurted out his question.

"I can't practice art at home, so I was wondering if I could do it here?"

"Oh dear, of course," she said, clearly concerned but still smiling brightly, "I could even give you lessons if you wanted!"

"That would be amazing!" Seth said, stunned, "Can we start today?"

She nodded, then started rummaging around in her desk for something. She walked over, and sat on the desk next to him, holding two scraps of paper in her hand.

"So, I'm assuming you decided to participate in the competition." she beamed.

"Yeah," he said shyly, "I mean, I know I probably won't win..."

"Don't underestimate yourself Seth," she said, smiling but firm, "You're one of the best artists I know, and I may be biased, but I would choose you over anyone else in a heartbeat. There's so much meaning to everything you draw, and it reflects how you act in your normal life. Your art holds your power that no one sees. Maybe not even you. Never lose that power Seth."

The bell started to ring, and Seth begrudgingly unwrapped the blanket from around himself. But as Seth grabbed his bag his teacher slid the two scraps into his hand, which Seth read immediately.

One was a newspaper heading from fifteen years ago, with the title:

Martha Volk wins scholarship to Prestigious art academy with scrap paper drawing

And the other was a blank piece of paper with his name written on it in sharpie that hadn't yet dried. Seth looked up, stunned

"You won this contest too?" he asked

"And I didn't think I could," she said mischievously, "our first lesson is right after school. Practice on that scrap during the day. It all starts with that. And if you ever need anything else, anytime, my doors are always open."

He nodded and stood up, making his way over to his own desk for the first class of the day. He was in good hands with people who cared. Now, even though the school was cold, inside he felt happy and warm and for the first time in a long time...he felt at home.

***

Seth walked into the art room after school. "Ms. Volk?" He said.

"Hello young boy with amazing art talents!" She said. A dress with paintbrush's all over flowed behind her.

"So are we starting your first art lesson today?"

"Yes." Seth replied.

Ms. Volk led Seth over to an art board and handed him some paints. "The key is to express yourself. There are no rules in art. let yourself run wild. Think of yourself being free."

"That would sure be nice." Seth murmured. He started painting an eye with flowers wrapped around it. "So priceless!" Ms. Volk gasped, seeing his art.

"Thank you. You and Hope are the only ones who like my art." Seth said.

"What about your parents?" The art teacher said.

"They aren't.... The I-love-your-art-so-much type. There more the I-just-wanna-give-you-the-evil-eye-and-put-your-art-in-the-trash type."

"Okay... I was thinking... would you maybe like to come over to my art studio tomorrow at noon?"

Chapter 10:
Return to the Water

As Hope comes hope from the doctor extremely happy that she will get to swim again and will get to do the thing that she was good at and that she enjoyed.

As her mom pulled out of the parking lot leading to the family's doctor's office, she was struggling to find an appropriate answer to reply to her mothers question. If she did go to the swim meet, would she even remember how to swim? I mean, she was the captain of the swim meets after all, so if she nearly drowned again, it would be highly humiliating. But if she declined the offer, she would be missing out on an opportunity she had been longing for all this time, AND letting her team down.

"I don't know." She told her mom, who she left waiting in suspense for too long.

"Well, you have to make a decision quickly! Your swim meet starts tomorrow and I have to confirm with the substitute captain if you'll be there to coach or not." Her mom insisted, who was eyeing the road with caution.

"What do you think then?" Hope asked her mom

"I think you should go, because you've been wanting to swim for so long! But wear a life jacket so the incident doesn't repeat." her mom Rachel suggested

"But the only ones that fit me are those pink adjustable peppa pig life jackets for toddlers!" She cried out

"You'll be more safe with a life jacket that fits you well! What happened at your last swim meet!"

"I almost drowned. BUT IF I WEAR THOSE LIFE JACKETS I'LL LOOK LIKE A BABY!"

"I want you to be safe, but I'm not going to go out wasting my money. You can do that." True, she could buy her own life jacket, but even wearing one would get her teased. She already got bullied by Zara once, and that was bad enough. Maybe she could buy the life jacket that was built into a swim suit so it wouldn't look so suspicious, but the high-tech ones were dead expensive, almost over 150 dollars! And she didn't have that kind of money to spend on her cowardness. She sighed and stared out the window which was passing a Mcdonalds. If only there was someone who could help her out at the moment... Someone like... "Nolan!" Hope cried out

"What about him?" Her mom surveyed her suspiciously

"Oh.. Did I say that outloud?" She asked, embarrassed at her sudden cry out.

"Sure you did! Are you mad at him or something?" Rachel chuckled.

"No no. It's nothing." Hope was silent for the rest of the car ride, turning down any of her mom's attempts at conversation. When they arrived at their house, Hope rushed upstairs to her brother's room who was sitting at his monitor, hands frantically moving across the keyboard to defeat a game.

"Can I enter?" She asked hopefully, crossing her fingers.

"Sure you can! I'm trash at this game anyways." A moan of defeat coming from the game followed this remark, as he switched to the home screen.

"So, what's up?" Nolan asked as Hope made her appearance in her tight black jeans and GAP hoodie.

"I need some advice. I have a swim meet tomorrow that I REALLY want to go to, but mom wants me to wear a life jacket to be safe."

"What's wrong with wearing a life jacket?" He asked with a disbelieving expression on his face.

"The only ones that fit me are those peppa pig life jackets and I'm NOT going to give Zara another chance to bully me."

"Well, maybe you could say to mom that you're going, but practise some laps in the pool now."

"Good idea. Could you supervise me? I know it's a weird question to ask and I am sixteen, but mom wont let me swim on my own now.

"Of course! Now get out, I'm changing." Hope obeyed, and quickly rushed to her room to pick out an outfit. She chose her white lace up two piece bathing suit with a tropical flower design printed on the front. She also picked out some light coloured jean shorts to wear over her swim-suit, put on a light brown sun hat with a black bow tied on front, and slipped her feet into some cute matching flip flops to go with her swimming suit which had a pine-apple to separate her toes. She was ready. Hope walked downstairs and opened the sliding glass door leading out into the backyard. She was immediately greeted by their pool, which was completed with a slide and a little diving board. In one of the sun chairs lay his brother, in his plain blue swimming trunks and light blonde hair reading the Percy Jackson series.

"Ready to swim?" He asked, hiding his worry.

"I'm actually kind of nervous, but let's just get this over with." Hope replied, releasing her elbow length hair and tossing the elastic aside with her shorts. She then positioned herself to dive, hands raised high above her head. She counted to three in her head, and when it was time, she pushed herself off the diving board and plunged into the water.

She had no idea which way was up, which way was down. All Hope was successfully doing right was flailing her arms left to right and jumping up and down in the water. She eventually found her head sticking over the surface, taking large gulps of air. Her arm which was now finally out of her cast was aching unbearably and she had to go to the side of the pool to rest it. Huddled up inside her fluffy white towel, her thoughts spilled out of her mouth before she could catch what she was saying.

"Will I ever be able to go back to the pool at this rate?"

"You forgot one thing. Normally before you start swimming you stretch. Why not try that?"

"Maybe, but my arm is already aching!" Are you sure it will work?"

"You tell me that. What did you say when I asked how stretching helps before swimming?"

"I said it does."

"Exactly." You could see Nolan's bright blue eyes peeking over the rim of his sunglasses, smiling. So Hope dropped her towel to the ground, jumped on a giant flamingo floaty which was cruising towards the middle of the pool, and began stretching. To be honest with you, it was helping a lot. Her arms were probably just so stiff from being inside that cast forever, so stretching them was a brilliant idea. After about five minutes, Hope retired to the pool and jumped in. The cool water sloshed at her side as she swam the length of the pool one stroke at a time. Loosening her muscles helped a surprisingly good amount, and she soon grew confident that she wasn't going to get teased. She got her brother to throw some spare goggles into the pool for her to retrieve, and her fastest record quickly beat five seconds. She quickly became confident that maybe Zara for once would be the one gaping at her.

Chapter II:
Breaking Point

Seth sat on the edge of his bed, drawing on his scrap paper. His first lesson had gone great, so everything seemed awesome. Well, everything except...

Seth looked out the window, wondering if Hope was looking up at the sky right now too. He liked to think that. Her swim meet would be starting about now though, so it was probably not so. His parents had of course forbid him from going, and the closest he had to a car was his drivers license and the one time a few days ago where he drove Hope to her swim practice in her MOM'S car. If only he had a car, then he would have been out of here months ago.

Thinking of getting out of this mess, he looked down at his scrap drawing. Mrs. Volk had said it was coming along nicely before he had left, so he was pretty excited.

And he thought it looked good too. He may not have had a car, but he had a power that no one would see until their jaws were on the floor.

He heard the front door slam shut with a diluted shout about him having to make dinner. His parents were going somewhere again. He wondered where somewhere was, but he probably didn't want to know.

He sighed and got up off of the comfort of his bed. His parents were awful, and the house smelled worse than ever before, but his room and even this apartment were his home and it would suck to lose it.

As he closed the door to his room, he heard one of the door hinges crack again and cringed. He genuinely pitied the person who would get this room if they ever left. He walked into the kitchen, holding his nose. He still remembered the fresh smell when they had first gotten to this place. It had been months since then. Months since moving, months since his first day at school, months since knowing hope. Everything felt like it was going so fast.

He went over to the refrigerator to see what food there was. There wasn't a lot, but it seemed like enough eggs for a breakfast dinner special, so he could make do. He put the eggs in a pan, and went over to clear the table, which his parents expected to be cleared when they got back for a dinner where they definitely didn't want him sitting with them(he'd learned that the hard way).

While he was digging through the piles of bills and old coupons, a part of a heading caught his eye. MAYFLOWER-it read, with a word clearly coming after it. Mayflower was the name of the town, so it was probably just another bill or "better" yet, a fine for breaking literally everything they touched. Yet something about this paper made him feel uneasy, and even though he knew all of the rules he was breaking by even looking at one of their papers, he picked it out of the pile and started reading. It was a letter.

Sent on April 22nd, from Mayflower Orphanage and adoption agency.

Dear Mr. and Mrs. Bradley,

We've reviewed all of the paperwork, and with one final signature at the bottom of this page, everything will be in order.

Well we are sure you are saddened by this decision, we hope this is better for your family's well being, and we will take great care of Seth until we find him a good home.

You can drop him off in three days at 451, Mayflower avenue.

```
Signed,
Justice Crale,
Director of the Mayflower Orphanage
and Adoption Center.
```

Justice Crale

Seth felt in that moment like the world had broken in half. He should have been unsurprised. They hated him. This was bound to happen at some point. And yet, some twisted, messed up, broken part of him still believed that maybe...maybe they still cared. They had put up with him for years after all.

NO! THAT'S NOT LOVE...THAT'S CRUEL!

He fell to his knees and started to cry. He tried to see but everything was a blistering, horrible red. Everything looked tainted and broken. He tore the paper in half without even realizing it. When he looked down and saw what he'd done, he couldn't even bring himself to smile. It wouldn't undo the damage. Nothing ever could.

He shoved the rest of the papers off the table and into a corner, his mind not able to process anything. He finished cooking the eggs and took some for himself, like he always did, still crying. His mind was so angry and red that his tears may as well have been blood on the floor. He toyed with the idea of keeping the fire on, just letting it all burn, but the last spark of sanity cried out in him, and he couldn't bring himself to do it.

He ran to his room and slammed the door, not caring how it splintered and cracked. As he seathed in a corner, trying to regain control, his eyes drifted over to the window... and the sky.

There's... still... hope?

Behind his hatred and burning, the sadness came flooding through. He collapsed on his bed and sobbed, not even sure why any more. He was still angry, still sad, he felt sick, not even able to bring himself to eat, but. . . a tiny part of him saw through that. A tiny part of him told him he wasn't alone anymore. A tiny part of him was... happy? No, not happy. It just realized there was still... hope. Heh.

After a while, he squeezed his eyes open. He had heard a click of ~~his parents~~ those people getting home a while ago, but other than that, he had no concept of time. He wasn't sure how long he had cried, but looking at his watch, it had been a few hours. Hope would be home from her swim meet now. It would take a while, but she stayed up late, so he could probably make it to her house on foot before she fell asleep. He could start walking now. Those people wouldn't notice...or care. He could just climb out the window of this tilted old building and run over to talk. They would talk for hours about what to do, and eventually they'd get a good plan. He wouldn't have to go anywhere, and he'd never have to come back to this awful place ever again… but he didn't. He still couldn't bring himself to uncurl from this ball he had curled into, let alone run 7 miles to get to an address he barely knew. There wasn't any hope left. He'd have to leave all his hope (literal and figurative) behind against his will because of **those people.**

He thought of all the time he spent with Hope. to the first day of school, to the day they met, to the day they became real friends, and the art class, the art class! The days she'd complimented his drawing, the day Mrs. Volk acted more like a mother than he'd ever known, the day hope brought cookies for mrs. Volk and he found out they were neighbors- Wait.

He didn't know which house she was in relation to hope. He didn't know her schedule, or if she was at home, or if she was even awake. But the idea of Mrs. Volk got him thinking. He sat up in bed, just realizing he was still holding the ripped letter. Maybe, just maybe…

He wasn't alone anymore, and he knew it. There were still people he could trust. All of his pain, his sorrow, his happiness, all the emotions he'd held back so long mixed together, and a look of determination spread across his face. He sat up, not smiling, not ok yet, but with a goal. He wiped his still wet face, with no tears left to cry. He turned toward the scraps of paper on his dresser. His spark. His power. Yes, he had a plan. He could get out of this… if he was patient.

***

It was Seth's second art lesson with his teacher and he had just figured out that his parents were getting rid of him. Usually, art class was his favorite part of the day, but today, it was worry city. Seth had the ripped adoption paperwork in his bag, he wondered if his mom and dad, yet noticed it was gone. Ms. Volk must of noticed his worries because she said

"What's bothering you today, Seth?"

"Uh... nothing." He said.

"It doesn't seem like nothing."

"Well. Maybe my horrible parents are going to send me away to get adopted." Seth said.

"See. That's not nothing." Ms. Volk said.

"Well I'm useless."

"No you're not."

"I'm getting adopted! By a total stranger! Yes I am."

"Maybe not a total stranger..." Ms. Volk said, flashing her mysterious smile.

"Well enough talk about that. Start painting." She said, handing Seth a smock and paints and paintbrush.

Ms. Volk took out her phone and started texting seriously. Seth tried to see what she was texting. The only words he saw was "Adopt Seth".

Chapter 12:
Diving and Thriving

As Hope's mom drives off to find a place to park and drops Hope off at the curb of her school she begins to get butterflies in her stomach with no motivation to go through with competing. Obviously her family and seth were but the rest of the school not so much as she stood there about to jump in the water Hope didn't freeze up she just felt incredibly weak. It was like one lap was to take her five minutes. Almost as if she was pulling a heavy anchor along with her as she was swimming. She lost so terribly she had to get out of the pool because one lap was talking too long and others had to compete in that pool. She felt humiliated enough but of course some people had some rude things to say about it. She is just coming off an injury so it is not realistic to think that someone is going to be immediately back to the same at their first competition. She is so stressed out with all these people expecting her to be perfect. She needs to calm down. She goes to the bathroom to fix her swimming cap that was so undone that the majority of her wet brown tangled hair was edging it way out of the cap. She starts to think that she probably shouldn't have had a pesto Starbucks panini an hour before the competition. She bolted to the toilet and began to throw up. Her nerves mixed with swimming and that sandwich did not go well. She eventually exited the bathroom and refused to go back in the pool and would just wait in her swimsuit until the competition was over.

Hope pressed her head hard into her fathers grey plaid shirt and her salty tears wetted his clothing but he didn't care. That's what Hope loved about her dad. He rarely cared about himself and made sure other people were OK first. She felt her mom's warm hand press into her back hugging her. She was glad that their reunion was in private, the thought made her feel safe and comforted.

"Shhh, shhh. It's ok, it's ok." Whispered her mother. Her head hurt, and her throat was tired from crying, but that didn't stop her from releasing all her feelings.

"I just want this all to end! Can I transfer schools?" She whined

"Honey, what about Seth? You're the only person he's got and he needs you!" Rachel pointed out

"Could I transfer schools with him? All I need is a fresh start!"

"Take this situation one step at a time, and it will be over before you know it." Her mother advised

"I just, It's just... Hard"

"Nothing that's worth getting is easy to retrieve. It's just the way things are." His dad cut in

"Then why can't I change the way things are?"

"You won't want to, because then the world won't be worth living for." Her dad explained. There was silence, and then her brother walked in holding a rock. It looked very special and unique, as it was the colour of forget me not blue and had designs of waves.

"A gift for you, to remember that you worked so hard to be good at swimming and you even started at the age of three! In life you have to work hard for the things you want, and later your work will pay off. You shouldn't give up swimming, you worked so hard to get good at it and you love it so much!"

"Thanks Nolan!" She smiled gratefully, revealing her puffy red face and taking the souvenir in awe. It had to be her favorite gift yet.

"Anytime!" He replied

"Well, I have to get back to the changing room now, thanks for your support." She kissed her parents on the lips and hugged her brother, then began walking away. She found the women's changing room easily as she had been in the gym countless times. When she walked in, Hope was greeted by Zara's gang, Victoria Wellson, Merrisa May, Ala Perkins, and Zara Macdonald.

"HOOPE! How was your swim meet?" Zara asked in a fake enthusiastic voice.

"Oh, I forgot. You forgot HOW to swim. You know, you were always terrible at it." Merrisa added, flicking her hair out of her face.

"I am not bad at swimming! Are you blind?" Hope failed to ignore them, and struggled to stay in control of her anger.

"You know, I think you were just scared because that freak wasn't there to save you. But I don't know. I don't understand the FREAK language." Victoria snarled.

"Good one Vicky. I've always wondered why you freaked out when I asked if you wanted to punch that freak. He was an easy target, but I guess you became an official FREAK after that."

"Zara, why would I want to punch my friend?" Hope's voice trembled continuously, and she clutched her chin to prevent it from trembling further and being in risk of making her cry.

"He's your friend? Wow! I didn't know such losers could possibly be so attractive." Ala smirked.

"YOU DON'T NEED TO BE ATTRACTIVE TO GET A FRIEND! YOU JUST NEED A GOOD HEART!" She was completely out of control, which she realized when she aimed a punch at Zara and missed. Hope returned to her swimming bag which felt unusually light.

"Looking for something?" Zara laughed and showed her a bundle of her belongings. Hope leaped towards her, but Zara had already tossed the bundle at Ala, who tossed it to Victoria, and Victoria threw it to Merrisa who flung it out the window into a dumpster. She was shocked, but it quickly turned to anger as she grabbed Zara's purse and flung it out the window after the bundle. Then with only her wet swimming suit and towel to keep her warm, Hope raced downstairs to retrieve her stuff. She could hear Zara's gang closing in on her heels, and she pushed herself to go faster. The door was just up ahead, if she could just reach it...

"ARRRGH!" She bumped into this man pushing a cart full of shot puts heading to the track and field area. The cart tipped over and the heavy balls were sent rolling in every direction. Hope pulled herself to her feet and dodged the rolling objects as she continued to retrieve her stuff. She burst through the doors into the outdoor world and felt her whole body shivering uncontrollably. But she had to continue. Ala who used to run in cross country events had an advantage from the cart as she also had the idea to keep going. She was now neck and neck with Ala, who was smirking at Hope, her ponytail flying backwards.

"Oh Hope. You really do have to work hard for the things you want in life, crybaby." Then she blasted ahead of her, but she had another thing on her mind. Had Ala overheard their conversation? Maybe they weren't in a private place afterall. But she had to catch up. She wasn't about to let Ala beat her again, like she did to Seth. The first day of high school, Zara's gang had noticed Seth before her which sparked a whole new fire. When the image of Seth flashed across her mind, she realized she was doing this for him, and he was counting on her. Somehow she found some energy hidden deep inside her, and she leapt in front of Ala and grabbed the purse plus her belongings.

"You give that back. You don't want the whole school to know you're a crybaby, do you?" She glared at her, with a mixed in horrified expression on her face.

"You don't want the whole school to know you were just in a dumpster, do you?" She repeated. As if on command, Zara, Merrisa, and Vicky arrived. They charged at Hope ready to tackle her, but just in the nick of time, she jumped out of the way and watched as they fell headfirst into a heap of mouldy cottage cheese, rotten fruit, and dog poop bags. All the new force added to the dumpster caused the lid to fall closed, locking them in darkness. Maybe she would wait just a little before pulling them out. After all the times Zara and her friends bullied her and Seth, she had gotten them back with their own evilness. Hope couldn't wait to tell Seth the story at school tomorrow.

***

It was 7:00 AM, and she woke up with tangled hair and a glum expression on her face.

"What's up, Hope?" Her mom asked, as she headed downstairs.

"Jus.. HUHH ...tired." She yawned.

"Well you better wake up, because you've got a math test at school today." Her mom informed, pushing a bowl of cornflakes towards her.

"I know. And, could you pass a spoon please?" Hope asked politely.

"Sure you can! Here you go." Her mom replied after she chose a large gleaming spoon from the cutlery drawer.

"Thanks." Hope took the spoon, and started shoveling cereal into her mouth. She looked up the latest trending videos on youtube and was surprised to see some familiar faces.

"Wait, it can't be! It's Zara! And that's Ala! And there's Victoria and Merrisa!" She said aloud, causing her mom to look over at her.

She clicked on the video, and began to watch it. It presented three stumbling girls tripping over shot puts as they attempted to pull themselves to their feet. One girl with sleek black hair appeared to be in pain, but she still followed the others out the doors. The video was now filming their backs, so it was hard to tell who they were. When they rounded a corner, she popped into the video as well as Ala and a green dumpster. She watched in secret satisfaction as the gang fell into the dumpster causing Hope to expect the video to be over, but it wasn't. The video editor put in a 20 minutes later text then it played again. This time four girls were climbing out of the bin, and all of them were in absolute MESS. Their shirts were smeared with greenish cottage cheese, their hair was tangled as heck holding banana peels and live worms. It was a disgusting sight, but also really funny. It got even more hilarious when Zara realized she was on video, and raised to the camera man with a don't-you-dare-film-me expression on her face. The video ended there, but she was filled with pride as the credits came up.

I GIVE MY THANKS TO HOPE HENDER-
SON, FOR CAUSING THE FOUR BULLIES TO
FALL INTO THE BIN. I ALSO WANT TO THANK
ZARA MACDONALD, MERISSA MAY, VICTORIA
WELLSON, AND ALA PERKINS, FOR TOLERAT-
ING BEING THE ONES DUMPSTER DIVING. FOR
MORE VIDEOS ON BIG FAILS, PLEASE LIKE
AND SUBSCRIBE TO MY CHANNEL! THANKS
FOR WATCHING!

She was a hero at school that day, apparently there were a lot more people who were bullied by the gang in the past. Seth for once had a good day, and lots of people honoured him as well for being Hope's friend. After the teachers figured out the four's wrong doings, they got a week's suspension from school and spent the whole of next week in detention. Things couldn't get better, and she was right. They could only get worse. The day after the video was published, Seth pulled Hope aside into an abandoned classroom. She was baffled, and couldn't hold a straight face.

"Stop looking so confused, Hope. I was just wondering, can you hold a secret?"

Hope knew that this was serious, and she automatically stopped smiling.

"What is it Seth?" She asked, expecting the worst.

"Well.." He looked down at the floor highly interested in a speck of dirt.

"What is it?" She was almost shouting now, and she shook his shoulders to bolt him awake.

"You see, my parents don't appreciate me at all and one night night while they were away I saw something."

"What did you see?" Hope was sick with worry.

"I saw... an adoption paper. I'm going to an orphanage." Seth was struggling not to cry, and he had to turn his back on her because it was impossible to look into her bright blue eyes.

"YOU CAN'T! I'll... adopt you!"

"Don't be silly, I'm not going anywhere unless you help me with something."

"What do you mean?"

"There's an art contest. And if I win, I go to a boarding school. Ms Volk has been giving me private lessons all week but I haven't got a chance to begin my actual painting."

"Why not at home?"

"You know what my parents are like... they think I deserve to go to an orphanage."

"Then come with me after school. You can stay overnight while we work on it."

"You sure?" Seth asked uneasily.

"Of course. My mom is always expecting this kind of stuff, she also won't mind if you go in the pool."

"You have a pool!" He gaped at her

"Maybe.." Hope smiled. So after a fun day with multiple fans following them around, Seth walked home with Hope after school.

"My brother has some clothes that don't fit him anymore that you can wear if you need to change into something."

"You sure?"

"Seth, look. The two rules at my house other than the usual stay safe ones are that you have to have fun and don't be shy. So DON'T break them."

"I promise I won't." He smiled ear to ear. When the two arrived at Hope's house, they munched on some home-made brownies and got to work.

"I was thinking that I could maybe draw a portrait of this black boy who kind of stands there with his legs wide open, hands balled into fists, and he's staring at his right foot.. He'll wear grey pants and have a faded hoodie." He drew a rough sketch of his idea and asked Hope if it was good.

"Is this guy resembling you? He sounds just like you. But I love it."

"Well, he's coming from me so he's got to sound a bit like me, right?" He defended himself.

"Well yeah. But what's the meaning behind the drawing?"

"Don't judge the amount of power hidden inside some people." He replied, and ripped out the sketch from his notebook and held it up so it caught the sunlight.

"It's perfect!" Hope hugged Seth, then quickly ran down to the basement to retrieve some art supplies. They agreed to sit outside as Hope practised some laps in the pool. And they went to work. After a while of Seth sitting alone under a table with an umbrella on the patio, Hope climbed out of the water and joined him.

"Wow." It really was a wowing drawing. Seth had added balls of fire coming out of his fists aimed at the ground.

Even though it wasn't done, she could still see it was going to amaze the judges.

"Seth, you deserve a break. Come join me in the pool." Hope didn't need an answer. Seth sprang to his feet immediately and went to their bathroom to change into Nolan's old swimming trunks which fit him perfectly. Seth arrived back in Hope's backyard and cannonballed right into the pool. When he jumped into the water, Seth's masterpiece, which was resting on a nearby table, got smudged severely by the water from the splash. After their fun, Seth was baffled and looked all over for his painting. Hope suggested he start on another one but it was a slow process. By the time they woke up the next day, Seth was in full on panic mode. Hope comforted him and suggested she look outside in the backyard one more time. But Hope was also worried sick. She would lose the only someone she had loved for a friend, and the thought of the orphanage alone made her want to barf. You would think that if she found the painting, Hope would be beyond happy, but wrong. She was horrified at her findings. What she showed Seth made his worry multiply as he stared into the once beautiful painting. You wouldn't be able to make out that powerful black boy as it was smudged beyond repair.

"Well?" She asked him

"Well what?" He snapped back.

"Well, where's your backup painting?"

"Here." He showed her something that looked like a fat flashlight with a ring at the top.

"That's the lantern you were planning?" She asked in disbelief.

"Yes! I only had ten minutes to work on it! What were you expecting?" What WAS she expecting? A perfect replica of the Mona Lisa? But no. Seth was a human being and his work wasn't perfect, but it was still surprisingly brilliant.

"Well, we should walk to school now so we're not late." Hope advised. She was still disappointed that their first sleepover was a disaster. She was also beyond scared of what would happen to Seth. How did he feel about the whole situation? Probably much worse. As they passed a bright green maple tree, Seth pointed it out to Hope.

"I could draw that!" He suggested.

"Yes, but what's the meaning behind it?" Seth was dead silent, then Hope up again.

"The judges will ask that question, you have to be prepared."

"I know! But now I'll submit anything other than that crap right now!"

"SETH! Don't talk to yourself like that! The colour is still, breathtaking." She pleaded

"Look, I have to submit a painting by 10:00 if I want to participate in the contest." He was right, there were no other options unless he wanted to rush it. So later that morning he submitted the painting to the judges and retired to Hope. They stared into each other's faces, saddened with grief. It seemed like there was no hope left.

Chapter 13:
And the Winner is...

One week had passed since Seth discovered the truth of the Mayflower adoption agency. Seth stared down at his finally finished drawing. It was an abandoned lantern in a forest. It was really good. All shaded and creepy. It would make anyone feel uneasy. Seth laid his head on his desk, sulking. On one hand, he was glad he hadn't submitted this to the art show unfinished, but gosh was this so much better than what he actually submitted to the art competition.

"Seth, pay attention kiddo" Mrs. Volk snapped her fingers in front of Seth's face, snapping him out of his sulk.

"I like that one." Seth said matter of factly, sitting up and starting to draw again, not looking at Mrs Volk, but a mischievous grin spreading across his face that was aimed at her.

"What do you mean?" Mrs. Volk asked, either playing dumb or genuinely confused.

"Oh come on," Seth said, looking at her smugly and throwing one arm over his chair, "Don't think I don't see what you're doing. You've been trying out different names for me all week. So either you're repeatedly mistaking me for different children, or you're planning something. And knowing you..."

He shook his head and chuckled. Mrs. Volk put her hands on her hips.

"Alright smart aleck," she teased, sitting next to him, "I see through you too you know. But I guess not as 'great' as you can. Wanna tell me why you've been in an art slump for the past few days? You look rested..."

Seth sighed, not wanting a fight. He pointed at the drawing on his desk, "Look at this drawing. What do you think of it?"

Mrs. Volk looked, thinking hard for a while, before saying, "the shading is really good, the light contrasts very well. It's very old-fashioned and creepy. I like it. Why?"

"Exactly!" Seth moaned, flopping onto his desk again and getting a weird look from Hope, who was across the room, sculpting, "it's so much better than the piece I actually submitted for the art show."

"Oh don't give me that Seth!" she said. this time, it was easy to tell what mood she was in as she was talking, "That drawing was incredible! It was abstract and colorful and gritty and happy and emotional and-"

"It was lines." Seth reminded her, trying not to give in to her overwhelming happiness.

"It was a reflection," the teacher reminded him, "of everything you've been through the past few days. They may have been lines, but they were powerful and determined lines. I know it, you know it, and...I think there are some other people that agree too."

She smiled mischievously, and went up to the front of the class to make an announcement. Seth pushed his chair out, ready for another encouraging speech to the "whole class". Instead, she pulled out a letter.

Seth's stomach flopped for a moment, remembering the letter a week ago- he shook that thought out of his head. It had been a week since that. Things were better now. He wished he could've stayed with hope forever, but of course he couldn't. Still, his first days at M.O.A.A were going great. He even managed to make a few friends. He wasn't normal, and he didn't want to be any more, but things finally felt...settled. He could still go to school, still hang out with Hope, still take art lessons! Zara and her gang were still popular, but he thought they were genuinely scared to bother them. He never had to worry about those people again.

"Attention class, we have big news!" she beamed, smiling into everyone's souls.

She paused for a second before continuing, "As you know, this art contest was an international chance at a scholarship. Everyone who participated had a very low chance of winning. And yet, I'm proud to say that for the first time in fifteen years, the winner has been announced to be someone in this class!"

Everyone cheered, and for a brief moment all seemed happy. And then the whispers started. Who had won? Who had gotten the scholarship? Who got to go and get a great education and not stay here in the "pits". Who would have to say goodbye to their friends and family?

"And the winner is..." Mrs Volk said, building up the suspense to the point of insanity. She opened the letter and her hand flew up to her face, then a happy smile spread across her face as a tear rolled down her cheek, "Seth? You won-"

Seth couldn't hear anymore, and everything was being muffled by Hope's sweater as she wrapped him in the tightest hug he had ever felt. Once she let go, Seth fell to the floor, and Hope cracked up, repeatedly trying to help him up, but constantly having to stop and clutch her sides. Everyone was looking at them either enviously or like they were crazy, and he'd be lying if he said he didn't care, but in the moment, all that mattered was hope. He rolled his eyes and pushed himself to his feet, trying to regain his composure. But the sight of hope still doubled over made him giggle, then snort, and then... he laughed. Genuinely laughed. Hope laughed with him, and soon he had fallen on the floor all over again, with hope beside him.

This time, it was Mrs. Volk who helped him to his feet, chuckling. She smiled at him, curious, and said, "you know, I don't think I've ever heard you laugh before..."

Seth stood there for a moment. Nothing could taint his happiness, but he was shocked at that comment. After a minute of thinking, he just took it as another victory. He had a secured future if he wanted it, a determined spirit, and most of all, he was finally...free. Free to complain, Free to joke, free to dream. Free to laugh. He finally felt like he was worthy of doing that, and other people would actually listen when he did. For the first time in a long time, Seth felt ok.

After the excitement had died down Seth began to worry. Hope, who was standing behind him on their walk to M.O.A.A, peered over his shoulder to smile at him again, only for her face to melt into confusion.

"Dude! You just won a scholarship! And the letter said that if you were younger, you could go there anyway and just spend more time! You'll never have to worry about this place again! Why do you look upset?"

Seth sighed and smiled tiredly, "because... because I'm dumb."

"UGH! Why do you still talk like that?" Hope said, Facepalming, "Seth, look at me. You're the kindest, smartest, bravest kid I know! What about that is dumb? You're. Not. Dumb."

"No, that's not the reason." Seth said, kicking at a pebble on the sidewalk, "I just- I know I should be happy right now! I just got this life changing opportunity, which is all I've ever wanted and more, but...I'm not happy. Because I'm dumb. Because... I don't wanna leave you guys. You're all I have."

"Oh. That's why," Hope said, trying not to smile, "Well, what would Mrs. Volk say?"

Seth sighed again, making Hope giggle, "Probably that I also have the power inside me, and that I can do this, and blah da de blah blah blah I'm a magical fairy prince. Happy now?"

Hope sighed, Giggling, "10/10, spot on, gold star. But that's not what I was thinking. What I meant was that you're not all alone when you go away. We're right here, just a call away. We'll always be here for you. No matter what you're doing or how far away you are. Because we love you Seth. And...if you don't want to go...no one's going to force you. You can't make my decisions, so I can't make yours. But Seth... don't let us stop you from fulfilling your dream. If this is what you want, Go for it!"

"You done monologuing yet?" Seth asked sarcastically.

"Ugh!" Hope whined, "Were you even listening at all?"

"Yeah, Yeah," Seth smiled, "Seriously though, Thanks. I think I needed to hear that."

"Any time," Hope said, messing up his hair.

"Aaugh!" Seth cried, laughing and covering his head as he ran down the sidewalk to M.O.A.A.

Hope ran after him, and they both made it there after a short time, panting and clutching their knees. Once Seth caught his breath, he turned to hope one more time.

"May I ask you something? I have one more problem I need to deal with."

"Alright, shoot!" Hope said, standing up fully again.

Seth bit his lower lip nervously, before blurting out, "The scholarship requires a parent or guardian signature!"

"Oh, well," hope smiled slyly, "We may have a solution for that too."

"Who's we?" Seth asked, tilting his head slightly.

"You'll see..." Hope said mysteriously, starting to walk away.

Seth shook his head, rolled his eyes, and went upstairs to start packing for a new adventure.

Chapter 14:
Finding Home

"Time for art class!" Seth practically sang. He loved art class. And his teacher. Seth walked in the art room.

"Hi Ms. Vol... what?"

Blue banners and streamers hung all around the room. Music was blaring from a beatbox. One big yellow banner said "Welcome to the family!" And there stood Ms. Volk next to a man who had a blue shirt that said "Seth welcome to the family" on it.

"Uhh..." Seth said.

The music ended.

"Seth, you are getting adopted by me." Ms. Volk said.

"What?!" Seth said. Tears were spilling down his cheeks. He ran over and hugged Ms. Volk. She hugged him back.

"I would like you to meet my husband, Dan." Ms. Volk said.

"Hi Dan."

"Hi Seth! How are you? I'm so glad you are part of my family now." He gave Seth a pat on the back.

"Congratulations Seth!" Hope came from the corner and hugged Seth.

"Thank you." Seth said felling dumb for not noticing Hope in the corner.

Ms. Volk came up and draped her shoulder over Seth. "Come on Seth, let's go home." she said. Seth was going home.

Seth wasn't surprised by how Ms. Volk's car looked. The shade of its purple matched her hair color perfectly. Flowers that looked so real and stunning like herself were all over the car.

Seth hopped in the back of the car. Dan drove and Ms. Volk sat in the passenger seat.

"You are going to love your room!" Ms. Volk said. When they parked, Seth saw that the house was blue. A soft blue. Paint smocks were stacked on a pink chair on the porch.

Ms. Volk opened the door and inside, the walls were splattered with all colors of paint and a bookshelf with no books but paints sat in the living room next to a lime green couch. Ms. Volk walked upstairs and Seth followed. She opened the door.

"This is your room!" Ms. Volk said. The room had blue walls and three easels aligned the walls, paints were scattered on the desk.

"I love it!!!!" Seth said. He flopped on the bed. It could probably fit five people. It was so big.

"I'm so glad you came to live with us." Ms. Volk said. "We had a son before but he... he... he wasn't the nice man we tried to raise him to be." Ms. Volk practically whispered.

"Well... I better make dinner. And I heard you won the art contest! I already sighted the sheet. I'm so proud of you!" That seemed like something a mother would say.

It was now night time and Seth changed into his newly bought pjs. They were soft on his skin. He went into his bed sheets and took a phone of his night stand. Dan was going to help him set it up in the morning. Seth put the phone back and tried to fall asleep. Nightmares were no stranger to Seth but this one was so scary. His evil mom and dad were hunting him and were going to hurt him. Seth woke up sweating. His alarm clock said 9:00 pm on it. Seth walked out of his room and walked to Ms. Volk and Dan's room.

"Could I... maybe sleep with you guys tonight?" Seth asked.

"Of course!" Ms. Volk said. Seth crawled in bed.

Seth didn't know if it was too soon to say it but he said it anyway.

"I love you guys." Seth said.

"We love you too... Seth." Dan said.

The warmth of Seth's new family brushed the nightmares away and put him to sleep.

***

Hope goes down to her garage to check the mail and as she is going through the small stack of letters she spots out of the corner of her eye a letter from UCLA. She began to go into a bit of a nervous frendzy. Once she calmed down she sat on the red futon in her garage. She took a deep breath, and started to rip the top of the white envelope getting some of the sticky goo from the envelope on her hands. She read the letter over and over again just to insure it was real! Hope was accepted by her dream college but it said on a swimming scholarship. She hadn't fully decided that she wanted to swim for the rest of her life. She knew that she wanted to swim in college but she also wanted to major in something that could make a difference in the world. From personal experience from seeing her good friend Seth go through this she decided that her difference should be something that could help kids like him who had to go through the adoption process. Her goal was to make as many kids as she could in a safe and happy home to live a great life with more opportunities. So she wanted to work at the adoption agency that Seth was adopted at. Just thinking back, Hope had learned a lot from her senior year. She really was able to find her true self of who she really was. Without getting injured she would have reached out and found new friends and new things that she enjoyed. Without meeting Seth she would have found her difference and impact in the world. Swimming was fun but Hope was thinking back and looking at how her future would be without finding that other half of herself that she didn't even know she had. She learned that sometimes things are truly meant to happen. And she just has to be patient in letting it happen!

Epilogue

Seth stared down into the photo and smiled. It presented Hope and him, who had been glued to together by their everlasting friendship. They had finally reached the last day of collage, and after their final celebration party which was one of the best days of his life, Seth had come to Hope's dinner for a friendsgiving with Seth's new parents Mr and Mrs Volk, and Hope's family. Seth walked into a bright room with a white double bed pressed against the far wall, white curtains drawn back letting peach pink light into the room. Propped against a window stood a white desk with many papers stacked on it. The fluffy lush carpet (I think you can guess what colour it was) reminded him of how he should wash up before dinner, as there was a big difference in colour.

"I love your new room makeover, but I should probably go fix my appearance before dinner." Seth complemented

"Thanks!" Hope replied from an armchair. He walked across the hallway and opened the bathroom door at the end of the hallway. When Seth turned the shower neauzel, hot water began gushing out raining on him as if it was a humid storm. Normally Seth was used to cheap showers which were unable to produce cold water as his old parents couldn't afford it. But this... well this was a big upgrade in life. The warm water reminded him of how he was now living a life he had once dreamed of but seemed so far away in a different universe. But when he went to middle school, the two universes collided, and he just managed to slip on to the other one before it floated away. A light call from downstairs told him dinner was on its way. So Seth turned the water off, slipped on a blue button up shirt and black trousers, then attempted to tame his hair (which never worked), and rushed downstairs. A strong smell of chocolate mousse and shepherd's pie filled the air and when he entered the room, he was greeted by a mountain of deliouses dishes waiting to be tasted. He snuck a blueberry into his mouth which was going to be put into a bowl full of other berries topped with whipped cream, and gasped. His teeth broke through the delicate skin and it exploded in his mouth. Seth racked his memory for the last time he tried a blueberry and failed. This must be his first time trying one, which was really weird. Seth drew a chair next to Hope and filled his plate with as many foods as possible without overflowing it (alouth it already was.

"Mmmm. This is so good!" Seth judged a brown ball truthfully.

"You like chicken balls? Oh thank you! It's a family recipe." Smiled Hope's grandmother.

"Really? Wow. How's it made?" He asked

"It's chicken skin coated with a sticky edible oil which makes the bread crumbs stick. It's filled with a special salad." She instructed. Before Seth could make another comment, Seth's parents rose and lifted their wine glasses.

"I make a toast to Hope and Seth, to wish them good luck as they embark on this new chapter of their life. Congratulations!" Seth's mom spoke up, looking directly into his eyes. Everyone repeated their names, then applause broke out from all around the room. The feeling was not happiness, not excitement, but something much larger. It was beyond any feeling of happiness, much more... immense. He bit into a chicken leg which held a mysterious yellow liquid inside it. He made Hope finish it as he wanted to try to strawberry souffle. I could go on all day and night, describing the looks and tastes of these foods, but let's not do that. Instead, when he felt his stomach about to burst at the seams, he stopped eating and took Hope in his hands and led her to the dance floor. There they danced until they could dance no more and stopped only when the sunset disappeared and a bright full moon announced it was midnight. Seth and Hope returned to Hope's bedroom early, but fell asleep extremely late. If they told their parents they spent most of the night by starting off talking about their futures, then ended up talking about climate change (somehow) they would probably get in trouble. But when Hope fell asleep resting her head against Seth's arm, Seth returned to his sleeping bag and propped her head against a pillow. It truly was a magical night, if you reflected on how much Seth and Hope turned their life paths around.

As Hope walked over to the table, her foot bumped against his bag, which spilled the contents everywhere. Old Homework assignments, a moldy sandwich or two, an award for one of his recent art projects. Seth groaned but smiled. He started to walk over to pick it up, and Hope rushed over with him, apologizing profusely.

"Sorry, Sorry!" she says, rapidly picking things up and stuffing them back in the bag. Nolan, Hope's brother came over as well, along with ~~Mr. and Mrs. Volk~~ Mom and Dad.

"So this is becoming a whole family affair then?" Seth asked, causing everyone to laugh. He smiled, then pulled out one of the miscellaneous pieces of paper from a pile. Seeing it, he smiled wider.

"What is it? Hope asked, trying to read over his shoulder.

"My adoption certificate," Seth beamed, remembering the day years ago when that had been set in stone, "best day of my life."

"Aww!" hope cooed, "read it!"

"Oh alright," Seth sighed. This happened every time he came home, " This is to certify that Seth A. Bradley has been formally adopted into the Volk family By Martha Volk, on June 24, 2014. And then there's the picture on the back but we don't have to look at that-"

Faster then the blink of an eye, Hope ripped the certificate out of his hand and flipped it over, pushing him away so that she could see it.

"Look how cute we were!" she said, leaving Seth to cringe in a corner as she walked around the room with it, "we should hang this up!"

"That's actually a good idea!" Nolan said, bringing over a thumbtack.

"Noooo!" Seth whined, "It's so embarrassing!"

"You've barely even seen it! Come! Take a look!" His mom said.

Begrudgingly, Seth walked over, only to be blindsided by a wave of emotions and memories. Standing in the front of the picture was a (very small compared to now) Seth, picking at the suit he'd clearly been forced into wearing. He was smiling but nervous. Hope was behind him. Putting her elbows on his shoulders, and resting her head on his (which would be impossible now considering how much seth had grown). Nolan was doing a peace sign off to the side as far as Seth could tell, but his figure was blurry since he was trying to get out of the sun. Mom and Dad stood next to each other on the other side, Dad's arm flung around Mom's shoulders. Hope's parents were sitting pretty far away, but you could still see them in background, Mrs.

Daniels' head resting on her husband's shoulder. Everyone was smiling.

It was a moment in time. A visual of how far they'd
come then, and how much more they'd done now. Looking at it for the first time in years, Seth felt a happy tear
rolling down his cheek, so proud of his younger self.

"Yeah ok, it's pretty awesome." Seth mumbled, trying
not to smile, only to burst out laughing when Hope leaned
under his low head and stuck her tongue out. Everyone
went back to their dinner, Hope and Seth being the last
to leave the picture.

"Seth?" Hope asked, looking up at him.

"Yeah?" Seth asked, smiling at his best friend.

"We made it. Through everything, we made it."

"I know." Seth said, squeezing her hand before sitting
down next to her.

"How's working at Mayflower going?" someone inquired
as they started eating.

"Great!" Hope replied, grabbing some food, "it's been
a bit busy with the last few weeks of college, but last time
I checked everyone was doing great. It's so nice to help
people."

"And swimming?" Seth asked, reaching for some food as well.

"Oh, OH!" Hope said, getting excited, "Now it's my turn to show you something!"

Hope stared at the gold medal she one. She was happy she won it at her college swim meet. Hope figured out that swimming wasn't her whole life. Seth said "what are you doing? I thought you said you were gonna show me something."

Hope showed and told Seth about the gold medal she won.

"Wow." Was all Seth said.

"I also got 94 kids adopted to good families in the last week! Oh yeah I forgot to tell you that I now work at the adoption agency!"

When Seth Hope comes back home from thanksgiving they are so happy to see each other. They did have some ups and down but they couldn't get through their senior year without each other. They start giving thanks and what they were both thankful for the most is their friendship. It wasn't something fake or pushed together they both truly care about one another and are so glad they had each other in the beginning they were both not so sure about one another but the universe kept pushing them together which ended up being the best thing that happened to them and they will all have each other for the long haul.

About the Authors

DANIELLA LAINEZ, is a rising 8th grader who is 12 years old born in San Francisco, California.
She attends Saint Veronica school, and has two older brothers. Some of her hobbies are volleyball, tennis, jewelry making, nail art, baking and drawing.

HANNAH GREGORY lives in Edmonton Canada where she continues to write stories. She spends most of her time reading novels, writing all sorts of plots, and spending her evenings at soccer practise on her Warriors club for U11 girls. She lives with her parents, sister, brother, fish, and dog and attends Westglen elementary. Hannah's favorite country in the world is England where her whole family on her dad's side lives. She absolutely cannot resist milk chocolate which is her all time favorite treat to eat.

RYANN STIDHAM lives in the city of Seattle with 14 pets. She is ten years old and published her first book on July 30th 2021. Her best friend is a dog named Princess. Ryann attended an online writing camp called Written Out Loud.

SARAMARIE WHITE is an avid reader, writer, and artist. As a proud member of the Allstars group, she has been called a Co - queen of writing, foreshadowing, and details. She often finds herself playing outside, making up imaginary worlds, hanging out with her family and friends (Who get to hear AAAALLLLLLLL about her upcoming writing project), or of course, writing! She currently resides in Bethlehem, New York, with her Mom, Dad, sister, and grandparents!